So This
Is the End

So This
Is the End

— *A Love Story* —

Alexandra Franzen

CORAL GABLES

So This Is the End: A Love Story

Library of Congress Cataloging-in-Publication number: 2018940706
ISBN: (h) 978-1-63353-788-0, (p) 978-1-64250-931-1,
(e) 978-1-63353-789-7
BISAC category code FIC044000 — FICTION / Women

Printed in the United States of America

This book is dedicated to Brandon.
I'm grateful for every day, hour, and
minute with you.

Table of Contents

Hour One

For the first twenty minutes or so, most people feel dizzy, parched, and disoriented. Others experience a flushed, frenzied feeling—like a feverish euphoria. But it's different for everyone. A small percentage of patients experience what doctors euphemistically describe as "a period of brief discomfort." Understatement of the century? Uh, yeah.

Currently, my "period of brief discomfort" includes jolts of searing pain in completely random places. My left ankle. The center of my forearms. The rims of my eyes. The fleshy connective tissue holding my hipbones in place. The soft underside of each fingernail.

The pain is so unbelievably intense, it's almost indescribable. The worst part is that I can't ask for help. I want to speak, but my throat feels paralyzed—like when you're dreaming and you're falling hopelessly off the edge of a skyscraper, or running to escape a pack of rabid wolves, and you try to scream but nothing comes out of your mouth. Not even the smallest sound. But I know I'm not dreaming. I know what this is.

A nurse wearing powder-pink scrubs pats my hand and encourages me to take a few deep breaths. Her voice is soft, her tone unconcerned. She's seen this scenario a hundred times before.

She coos, "Just a few more minutes. I know, I know, it's no fun, but you're doing great. This is totally normal. I know, I know . . ." and keeps patting my hand. *Pat, pat, pat.*

I focus my eyes on the clock mounted onto the hospital wall and I will myself to breathe. One small sip of air every few seconds. *Tick, tock, tick.* The second hand moves hypnotically inside its glass cage, one notch at a time. Black hand. White clock. Beige wall. Speckled tiles. I wonder how long I've been conscious. There are no windows. I wonder if it's morning or night.

Warmth spreads across my body, and I feel something shift inside of me. Muscles loosen. Neural pathways reignite. The nurse checks the dilation of my eyes.

"Do you think you can sit upright? How about a few sips of juice?" she asks.

I nod. She offers me a small plastic cup of orange juice, and it tastes like seaweed, egg yolks, and black licorice. It's all wrong. I wince and try to spit it out, but my face doesn't cooperate and now it's dribbling down my chin. Humiliating. She smiles kindly.

"Taste is one of the last senses to return," she explains. "But don't worry, all of your vitals look perfect.

Just give it a little more time. You're almost there. Try to stay relaxed, and don't move your left arm, OK?"

She gestures towards my arm, which is hooked up to a massive electrolyte drip. "The doctor will stop by shortly for your exit examination."

She pads out of the room in her spotless white sneakers. There's a metal tray to my right, and I set down my glass of undrinkable juice, switching to water instead. It tastes like water is supposed to, which is a considerable relief. I gulp as quickly as I can, letting it lubricate my raw, cottony, aggravated throat. Happily, my facial muscles cooperate a bit better this time. No dribbling. I down the entire glass. I feel like I could drink forever.

There's the most god-awful taste in my mouth, and it's not from the juice. It's my own breath. It's a horrible stench. Rotten. Deathly. Like I just smoked a moldy cigarette and washed it down with a can of oily sardines and stale corn chips. The water helps a little. Not enough. Note to self: find a toothbrush as soon as humanly possible.

I gaze at the wall-mounted clock once again, finding it oddly soothing. The second hand moves rhythmically—pulsing forward, unendingly, like the ocean lapping the shore.

There's a reason for all of this.

A reason why I feel like human garbage. A reason
why there's an IV needle piercing my left arm. Why
I'm waiting to be examined by a doctor in a room I've
never seen before. Why I'm lying here, semi-paralyzed,
gradually regaining control over my body.

I chose this.

This is my "bonus round."

An extra twenty-four hours of life, even though I've
already died. "Temporary Cellular Resuscitation" is the
official medical terminology. TCR for short.

I've been resuscitated—successfully, it appears—and
now I have approximately twenty-four hours to do
whatever I want. Call my mom. Say goodbye to friends.
Make amends. Watch the sunset one last time. You
know, wrap things up with a nice, tidy bow before my
body wilts and I die again a second time—permanently.
Because that's how it works. After you die a second
time, that's it. It's fully and completely over. You don't
come back. There is no third chance. Hence the word:
"Temporary."

TCR is pretty expensive. Health insurance doesn't
cover it because it's considered an elective procedure.
A luxury—like laser hair removal or teeth whitening—
not a necessity. Some people think it's frivolous.
Conservative religious types think it's tampering with
God's plan. Most people think it's an unnecessary
expense or simply can't afford it. Some, I suspect, could

afford it but choose not to invest because they don't want to think about dying—let alone dying twice. Bottom line: most people don't purchase TCR.

Apparently, I'm not most people.

As soon as TCR was approved by the FDA, I leapt at the chance to purchase it. I honestly can't explain why it appealed to me so much. Curiosity, maybe. Fear. Both. I don't know. Who knows why anybody wants anything they want? I just knew that I wanted—needed—this procedure. A chance to rebound from death back to life? Sign me up. I couldn't really afford it, but I impulsively made the purchase anyway.

I called the TCR agency located closest to my home—I searched on Yelp first, of course, and it got terrific reviews, almost entirely five stars—and I spoke to a cheery, somewhat robotic customer service rep.

She asked for my birth date, home address, social security number to automatically notify the IRS in the event of my death ("One less loose end for your loved ones to tie up!" she explained enthusiastically), the name of my primary care physician, family health history, and all the other pieces of administrative minutiae that you would expect.

"Would you like to make a series of three payments, or shall we take care of your entire payment today?" she asked me in a thoroughly rehearsed fashion.

All of it, I confirmed. I paid the $9,999 fee with my American Express Gold Rewards card, maxing out my limit. The sales rep explained that I'd receive an email confirmation note within minutes, and that I'd be entered into a nationwide database so I could receive the TCR procedure at any hospital, anywhere in the United States.

"Except Hawaii and Alaska," she added. "Though we are working diligently on expanding our coverage base."

Awesome. I can die almost anywhere I want, I remember thinking morbidly. Such a convenience.

"Thank you for your purchase today. On behalf of everyone here at the Timeless Moments TCR Clinic of Minneapolis, I'm wishing you good health, and I hope you won't need the service you've purchased for a very long time."

"Me too," I replied. That was the end of our conversation.

I died at my local hospital less than three years after that phone call. I was thirty-two years old. Or should I say, I *am* thirty-two years old? I guess today, the answer is: both.

I know it sounds so cliché, but it hasn't really settled in that I'm dead. It doesn't feel real yet. I thought I'd have more time. A lot more time. I guess almost everyone thinks that.

I'm feeling lightheaded, and I wonder if that's another TCR side effect. Seems pretty likely.

TCR is a pretty crazy procedure—like something out of a sci-fi movie. Every cell in my body has been artificially revived with an intense electric shock, plus an influx of fresh plasma and electrolytes, plus an intrathecal injection. So, imagine a giant needle filled with epinephrine—pure adrenaline, basically—pumping directly into your spinal column. A flood of synthetic, lab-generated hormones flooding your body combined with that lightning snap of electricity and *Zow!* You're temporarily back in action. Like Frankenstein's monster, but without the green skin and those weird plugs on either side of your neck.

And here I am.

This is Hour One. The very first hour of my twenty-four-hour bonus round. I paid for it—now it's my time to use however I want.

Obviously, I want to make the most of this extra time. I want to maximize every minute.

Unfortunately, there's no guarantee that I'll get exactly twenty-four hours—that's more of an average guideline. Around hour twenty-three, most people start to fade. Fainting. Wobbling. Progressive organ shut down. It could happen sooner. Or you might be one of the lucky ones and get past the twenty-four-hour mark.

They say this one guy in Croatia made it to twenty-nine hours and fourteen minutes. That's the record.

Some experts claim that stress-relief techniques— like meditation, or even a glass of red wine—can help to extend the TCR timeframe and help you eke out a couple of extra minutes, maybe even an extra hour, but who knows? New studies are being done all the time and the findings never seem consistent. The only thing that's certain is that TCR provides a second chance at life, but pretty quickly, the ride is over. There's a big, fat period at the end of the sentence, not an ellipsis.

I glance at the clock. Is it my imagination, or is the second hand moving at double-speed? I feel flushed with urgency, itching to get out of this bed. Where is that damn doctor?

I am thirty minutes into my bonus round, and I've done basically nothing except feel uncomfortable, pathetically choke down some water, and stare at the clock on the wall. Jesus. Not exactly a rip-roaring start to my last day on earth.

My phone is resting on the tray next to my half-finished juice. I should call my mom. Except I have no idea what to say.

"Hi, mom, I'm dead ... but I'm sorta-fake-alive for about a day, so I figured I'd call ... uh, how's the retirement center? Are they serving Jell-O tonight?"

Yeah, no. I'm not emotionally ready for that phone call just yet. Maybe in a few hours.

I flip through my phone to the Memo section where I jot down notes and reminders. I know I've got a list in there called "bonus round," filled with all the things I told myself I would definitely do on this very special day.

"Eat a cheeseburger." "Pet a puppy." "Dance like nobody's watching."

It's a long list filled with all kinds of obvious stuff like that. Dance like nobody's watching? Seriously? That's the best I could come up with? None of it feels important anymore—and time is running out.

What is taking the doctor so long?

Exasperated, I down the rest of my juice. It tastes like oranges should. So that's good.

Maybe I should check Facebook.

Hour Two

The first thing I do is change my Facebook status to "Remembering."

That's Facebook's polite way of indicating, "This person is dead—let's remember them fondly, shall we?"

I prop myself up and angle my phone from above so I can take a hospital bed selfie. As usual, it takes about fifteen tries before I get a decent looking photo. I tweak the color saturation and add a filter to make myself look a little more vibrant, a little less gross. Then I post the photo along with an update:

So ... I died.

I pause, weighing my words carefully. What are you supposed to say in this type of situation? How do you announce your own death to hundreds of semi-friends?

Remember that weird thing that was going on with my heart, guys? The crazy-fast beating and fluttering feeling?

Well, as some of you already know, I was diagnosed with genetic arrhythmia, and I went into surgery for a catheter ablation. (That's a fancy term for: doctors using lasers to cauterize the rogue cell that was causing my heart to beat irregularly.)

Ablations are typically a really safe procedure. Super high success rate. 99.4% of patients get through it with no problem. .6% don't make it. I was one of the .6%.

Turns out, I died due to a complication with the anesthesia. Some type of freak allergic reaction to the drugs or something. They didn't even have a chance to begin the surgery. I died before they even cut me open.

I pause again, wondering how I know all of these specific details about my death.

Was I briefed by my surgeon at some point? I don't remember that conversation. Yet the information is flowing out of my fingertips, and I know each word is one hundred percent accurate, but how could I know all of this? I was unconscious throughout all of it. At least, I think I was. Or maybe some part of me was conscious the whole time, watching from inside, or from outside my body? Watching from above?

It's too weird to process the implications of what that could mean, so I focus my attention back onto Facebook. I keep typing.

So that's how I died. I guess I should feel shocked, or upset, but it hasn't fully hit me yet ...

Maybe I'm "oversharing." Is Facebook the right place for this type of announcement? Do my online friends and acquaintances really want to hear all of this? I'm aware that it's kind of a bummer. Also, how do I finish up this post? Maybe something like:

This is your sorta-dead friend, over and out, you may now return to your baby photos, engagement rings, and cat memes?

Uh, no.

I drum my fingers for a few moments, trying to think of some type of witty closing statement. You know. Probably the final words I'll ever write. No pressure or anything.

I settle on this:

I'm doing my "bonus round" right now. Struggling to think of things to do with my time. I've got about twenty-four hours before ... you know. Any ideas?

I post the update and lean back in my hospital bed. I refresh the screen.

Jesus Christ. So many comments. Such a big reaction, more than anything I've ever posted before. Everyone has an opinion on what I ought to do with my bonus round. Well, I did ask.

Watch the sunset ...

Go bungee jumping ...

Eat a TON of chocolate ...

Dance like nobody's watching ...

The list goes on and on. Dozens of well-intentioned suggestions. Maybe even hundreds. But for some reason, all of the encouraging words just make me even more frustrated and depressed. Also: why is everyone obsessed with dancing like nobody's watching? Who decided that's the "thing" to do to before your time on earth is up? Oprah? Deepak Chopra? The cast of *Dancing with the Stars*?

I know my friends are just trying to help—but it's not helping. They don't get it. Nobody gets it. Not a single one of my friends can understand what this feels like—this feeling of absolute finality. Knowing that time is, quite literally, running out.

I Google "Ideas on what to do during your bonus round" and find numerous blog posts with titles like "31 Helpful Tips For Your TCR Experience" and "100 Final Day Ideas! (#23 Will Seriously Blow Your Mind!)." I click around for several minutes, lulled into the glow of the screen, and then it hits me:

I'm nearly two hours into my bonus round—and all I've done is check Facebook and click through a couple of Google search results.

This is how I'm spending my final day on earth? *This* is my grand finale? A sickening feeling pools in my stomach, something between shame, embarrassment, urgency, and genuine terror. No. This isn't how it's going to go down.

I need to get out of this hospital.

As if on cue, the doctor arrives to examine me. Finally. Any longer and I might have ripped the IV drip out of my arm myself.

He nods at my chart, listens to my heart, and taps
both of my knees with a tiny plastic hammer. He asks
if I can stand up, if I can yawn for him and say *ahhh*, if
I remember my name and what year it is. Everything's
all good. Thumbs-up. He scribbles a few notes on a
clipboard and then gestures to a table where some fresh
clothes are laid out for me to change into. But he's not
quite finished yet. "Just one last thing . . ."

He shows me an app on my phone that will track
my movements and send an ambulance in case I need
assistance at any point.

"Assistance" is a euphemism for: pick up my failing,
crumpling body if I don't, can't, or won't return to the
hospital in time for my second death.

"But don't worry too much about that, OK? Just
enjoy yourself," he urges me. "I hope this special day
is everything you, ah . . ." There's an awkward beat.
"Everything you had hoped it would be."

A flash of pity crosses his eyes, as if he's just now
realizing my "condition." As if he's seeing me for the
first time. I wonder, momentarily, if he has a son
or a daughter and how old she might be. My age?
Younger? Older? Does she look like me? I wonder if he's
wondering how much time she has left. Or how much
time he has left. Nothing like staring death in the face to
abruptly remind you of your own mortality.

"Do you have kids?" I ask.

He nods. "Two."

"Please tell them you love them. Today."

His eyes mist over and I know I've struck a raw nerve. My eyes fill with tears, too, and I reach out instinctively to take his hands into mine. He doesn't protest. We say nothing.

The second hand moves around the clock. Full circle. For one minute, we are not doctor and patient. We are not separate. We are two human beings awash with immense emotions--feeling the urgency of life, the unfairness of death, the agony of loss, the mystery of it all.

I want to say something profound but it feels like … there's just nothing to say. So we just exist there, on the brink of words but ultimately saying nothing. His hands rest inside mine. I can feel the warmth of his skin, the smooth underbelly of each finger pad. The hands of a man who works long hours doing delicate, precise things. I don't think I've ever held a stranger's hands before. Not since being a kid on the playground.

"OK, OK," he mutters gruffly after another few more seconds have passed. Pressing away his tears with a flattened palm, he composes himself. "It's time for you to get out of this hospital. What are you going to do first?"

"I don't know," I reply. "I have no specific plans. I guess anything could happen."

He nods and moves towards the doorway. For a moment, it seems as though he's gathering his thoughts--preparing, perhaps, to offer me a small piece of advice, or a few words of comfort. But just then, there's a commotion in the hallway outside.

A stretcher is being pushed frenetically down the slick flooring. There's a blur of pink, blue, and green scrubs and a voice delivering clipped orders in rapid succession. The doctor's pager buzzes. He glances at it and then slips into the hallway, speed-walking in the direction of the stretcher, moving along to his next patient—living, dead, or somewhere in between.

I'm alone.

I'm guessing this means my exit examination is over, and apparently I … passed. I gather my clothes and race against the clock, seeing how quickly I can get dressed and get out of this eggshell-colored medical tomb. My shoes are laced and double-knotted, and I'm ready in just ninety-two seconds. Not bad.

I grab my phone and head for the door. The rancid taste in my mouth has finally dissipated. The jolts of pain are gone. No more paralysis. My body is my own again. I feel electrified. Better than I can ever remember, actually. Sharp. Alert. Intensely alive.

I walk past the registration desk. Nobody stops me or asks me to sign any paperwork or anything, and everyone looks very busy, so I just keep going. I walk quickly through the waiting room filled with the scent of anxiety and impatience, through the double-paned glass doors that part automatically, and into the stark brightness of the city.

I have no idea what happens next.

I guess it's all up to me.

Hour Three

When was the last time you looked at the sky?

I don't mean "to snap a photo for Instagram." I don't mean "to check if it's raining."

Can you remember?

I almost don't remember how to exist without a phone attached to my hand, hip, or ear.

I almost don't remember how to experience the world without needing to document, upload, or comment upon every waking moment.

For a few minutes, I try to remember.

I sit on a bench outside the hospital and just look at things. People. Clouds. Cars. Gurneys being wheeled in. Wheelchairs being wheeled out. Couples reuniting.

A girl on crutches hobbles out with her tall, lanky boyfriend's arm around her waist. He supports her as she fumbles like a newborn fawn, hesitantly hovering her bandaged ankle above the ground. Her face twists into a mask of concentration. She's doing her best not to trip over her crutches or place any pressure on her injured leg. Her boyfriend—or husband, whatever—is looking at her with the most intense look of adoration I've ever seen on a human face. He loves her. He loves her so goddamn much. It's obvious.

She hobbles over to their car. He helps her into the passenger seat, stores the crutches into the trunk, hops inside and leans over to kiss her. Long, slow, and deep. His fingers rummage through her hair. She smiles with her eyes closed. They drive away, and I get the feeling he's driving extra-slowly and cautiously because he wants to demonstrate that her safety and comfort are his utmost concern. *Precious cargo onboard.* It's such a subtle thing, such a small gesture of thoughtfulness and care, but it kills me.

I feel a violent, stinging pang of loneliness in my chest—so sharp and unexpected, I almost cry out in pain.

Watching this couple drive away from the hospital cul-de-sac, I'm hit with an overwhelming desire to toss my phone into the garbage.

I know it's odd. I know it's careless and rude. I know I won't be trackable by the hospital—which will be highly inconvenient for them in, oh, about twenty-one hours when I expire for the last time and my body needs to be collected. I know, I know, I know.

But it occurs to me that I haven't been more than twelve feet away from my phone in about twelve years. I literally sleep with it less than a foot from my face. I always have.

These are my final hours on earth. I want to be untethered. I want to feel free. Most of all, I want to feel completely awake. No digital distractions. There's a garbage can right by the entrance to the hospital and so, down it goes. My $999 iPhone X lands on a crumpled sandwich wrapper and that's that. Bye.

I stand up and stretch my arms into the air—one of those big, epic stretches like when you're waking up after a long nap. I feel like my fingertips could touch the sky. I feel strangely light, almost like I could float. Probably because I haven't eaten anything since … well, since the day before I died.

You know what?

I'm getting that cheeseburger after all.

Hour Four

"Oh my god," I mutter to nobody in particular, closing my eyes and swooning in ecstasy. Best. Cheeseburger. *Ever.*

It's a soft pretzel bun—perfectly buttered and toasty—piled with crisp lettuce that makes that pleasant *crrrunnnch* sound when you bite down. A perfectly grilled hamburger patty, scorched around the edges, medium-rare inside, nestled atop some kind of garlicky, creamy, miraculous sauce. Pickles. Tomatoes. Caramelized onions. Plus sharp cheddar cheese and (because screw it, I'm already dead) three strips of thick-cut bacon.

I arrange myself in a booth near the window. The waitress brings my burger along with a side of sweet potato fries dusted with chili powder and salt.

"Refill on your drink?" she asks.

I nod and smile like a kid on Christmas morning, reveling in the perfection of this moment.

Light pours through the glass, and the ice cubes in my drink twinkle like stars. The fizzy sweetness reminds me of being a little girl, riding my bicycle with my dad around the lake in Loring Park. We had a Saturday morning routine: bike ride followed by deep-fried cheese curds—my favorite snack as a kid, because they squeak in your mouth—and ice-cold Dr. Pepper. After that we'd usually browse through stacks of twenty-five cent comic books—all laid out in bins on the boardwalk. He was a DC comics guy. DC all the way. Not Marvel. He was my real-life superhero, so obviously I was a DC girl, too.

We'd have long, intense discussions—well, as "intense" as a conversation between a six-year-old kid and a thirty-six-year-old man can be—about who would win in a battle: Batman or Superman.

"Batman would lose!" I'd insist. "He doesn't have any superpowers. Just a bunch of fancy cars and stuff."

"Oh, I don't know about that," my dad would wink. "You're forgetting that Superman has a fatal weakness."

"Kryptonite?" I'd say.

"Not Kryptonite . . ." he'd say. "Kryptonite weakens him, but there's always an antidote. That's not his biggest weakness."

"So what is it then?"

"Love."

Superman loves Lois Lane, and he will do anything to keep her safe. Love makes him strong, but it can also bring him to his knees, ruin him, make him insane and irrational, compel him to bend the laws of science and defy the natural order of things. To save Lois Lane's life, he'll do anything. Even put the fate of the entire human race in peril.

I remember one issue where—after Lois dies—Superman uses his super-strength to turn the earth backwards and reverse time to find her so that he can change history to prevent her death. It works. But there's a cost. I read the issue so long ago, I don't remember how it all plays out. My dad would remember. He remembers details like that.

Remembered, I correct myself. Past tense.

The final quarter of my burger is looking less and less appealing, and the fries have gone cold. I push the plate to the edge of the table.

Yes, dad died. Yes, I could have spent more time with him before he passed. No, nobody could have predicted that he only had six weeks to live when the doctors said six months. No, it's not helpful to punish myself for not being at his bedside to hold his hand at the moment he passed. Two different shrinks, one life coach, and basically every single issue of *O: The Oprah Magazine* told me that in order to "live my best life," I need to forgive myself and move on. But hearing that advice from seventeen different sources doesn't make it any easier to follow.

Tears splash onto the Formica table, and I fight to keep myself contained. No sobbing. I don't want to make a scene. I rub my eyes with the back of my hands, and my hospital bracelet scrapes my skin.

I flag down the waitress and ask for a pair of scissors to slice it off. The waitress nods like it's not a peculiar request in the slightest, certainly not the worst one she's heard today. She brings over a pair of scissors along with my check.

I cut myself free. Leave her a twenty-dollar tip. Collect myself. Step outside and resolve to do something I should have done about four hours ago.

Call my mom.

Hour Five

There's a pay phone outside the restaurant that's so neglected and grimy, it looks like it's been pulled from the depths of a prehistoric tar pit.

I have serious doubts about whether or not the phone is even going to work. It probably hasn't been used in about seventy-million years. I'm stunned when I pick up the earpiece and—miracle of miracles—hear a dial tone. The thing is alive. I insert all the loose change that I have, dial one of the only phone numbers that I've ever committed to memory, and wait.

Seven rings, and finally . . .

"Yes?"

The voice on the other end sounds hesitant and unnerved, as if she's not quite sure whether she just received a call, whether she just called somebody else, or whether all of this is a dream.

But beneath the fog of dementia, there's a fierceness and fire that is unmistakable. It's the fire that got my mom through the loss of her first child, my older brother, whom I never got to meet. It's the fire that got her through my dad's cancer and the financial ruin that came in the wake of his illness. It's the fire that compelled her to throw a glass of water directly in my first boyfriend's face after he brought me home from a date three hours late. He ran from our doorstep, sopping wet, mumbling ineffective apologies. I have my suspicions that it may have been rubbing alcohol, not water, in that glass. She did not confirm … nor deny.

My mom is the strongest woman I know. Twenty times stronger than me. But all the grit, spit, and vinegar in the world couldn't save her from the suffocating onslaught of Alzheimer's.

A few years ago, she and I both agreed that putting her into an assisted living retirement facility was the best option for both of us. She always wanted to retire near the ocean, not be landlocked in the Midwest, so off to California she went. Her mental state declined steadily after moving into the Sunset Palms Senior Living Center in San Diego. I call weekly, and the odds are fifty-fifty that she remembers who I am. "She has good days and bad days," as her caregiver puts it.

"Hey mom," my voice cracks with emotion. "It's me."

"Sweetheart!" she says.

I choke back a sob. Today is a good day.

"How are you?" she asks me, and I can imagine her sitting in her favorite silk kimono, her hair in those rollers that she's used for the past sixty years of her life. I'm guessing the white peonies that I sent over for Mother's Day have been arranged in a vase by her bed. Her nails are probably painted peach-pink, not a single chip or ding in the polish, because a woman's got to have her standards, after all. She taught me that.

"Good, mom, I'm good," I say. In this moment, it feels mostly true.

"And how is that sweet boy? The professor?"

I shake my head. This. Again. The storyline she cannot keep straight.

"Mom, Kevin and I broke up over two years ago," I repeat calmly, for probably the millionth time.

"Oh," she says, her voice saturated with surprise and concern. "He was such a nice young man. I'm sorry things didn't work out."

"Yeah, mom, actually … I broke up with him," I say. "We just weren't compatible. But we're still friends, sort of, I guess. It's all good."

"All good," she repeats, as if the combination of words feels strange on her tongue. Her voice shifts into a saucier tone. I can practically see one eyebrow cocked.

"So," she continues. "I suppose there's no possibility that I might be getting a grandchild for Christmas this year?" she asks coyly. "Not even just one?"

I laugh. When it comes to her desire for grandkids, she is absolutely shameless.

"Mom, I . . ." I pause, realizing the finality of what I'm about to say. "That's definitely not going to happen."

"Well, ohhhkay," she sighs theatrically. "Go ahead and break your mother's heart."

I wince. Bringing even a single minute of suffering into my mom's life is the last thing I want to do. Which means, obviously, I shouldn't tell her the real reason I'm calling.

"You still there, darling?" she asks, and I realize I've been silent for several beats.

"Yeah, momma," I say, trying to swing into a change of subject. On impulse, I ask:

"Mom, looking back on your life, what has been your greatest regret?"

There's a long pause. I hear the sound of violins in the background. My mom's favorite classical music station—the one she keeps on practically 24/7 these days. It's Vivaldi's *Four Seasons.* One of her favorites.

"I … I don't understand," she half-stutters, and her tone is like a child lost in a crowded shopping mall, asking, *"Have you seen my mommy?"*

I sense her slipping away from me. The disease rolling in like a bank of fog across the shore.

"Yes? Who's calling?" she says. "Hello?"

No no no, mom. Don't disappear. Stay with me. Panic seizes my gut.

"Mom, it's me. It's your daughter. It's Nora. I wanted to ask you … I know this is a weird question, but, if you only had a few hours to live, what would you do? Like, what would you do with your time?"

There's another long pause, and I drum my fingers nervously along the spine of a battered phonebook. Come on, come on. Don't leave me, mom.

"Chocolate cake, champagne, and multiple orgasms," my mom replies confidently. "Possibly all at once if time is running short."

She's back.

I laugh and press the mouthpiece of the phone close to my lips and cheek, as if somehow I can press hard enough to transport myself to her room.

"But why would you ask a question like that?" she titters, joining my laughter.

"Mom ... I love you," is all I can say in response.

"I love you too, my darling. When are you coming to visit again? Next month?"

My stomach twists into lead.

"Mom, I . . ." I don't want to lie, but I don't want to tell the truth either. I settle for: "I don't know."

"Well, when you know, you let me know."

"I will."

She yawns deeply, and I hear a subdued knock in the background. Muffled voices. Clinking glasses.

"Sweetheart, it's time for afternoon tea and then a nap. You'll call me tomorrow, yes?" she asks.

I could be imagining it, but I swear I can hear just the subtlest hint of anxiety in her voice—like deep down, beneath the brain-fog, some hyper-intuitive part of her mom-psyche knows that there will be no call tomorrow.

I don't want to answer the question. Instead, I say one last true sentence:

"I love you so much, mom."

"I love you too, darling."

I love you.

Three words that are so much better than "goodbye."

I hang up. I imagine her sipping her tea, cozy and serene in her bedroom, and I feel so grateful that I got her on the phone, that she was lucid, and that today was a good day.

For one wild, illogical moment, I consider purchasing a plane ticket and flying to see her in San Diego. I run through the mental calculations. An hour to drive to the airport. An hour for checking in and getting through security. Four hours in flight, assuming—best-case scenario—that I can book a direct flight that leaves immediately with no delays. Two hours battling rush-hour traffic to get to the assisted living home. Eight hours of travel-time, minimum. More like ten or twelve, realistically.

By the time I arrive, she'll probably be asleep. Even if she's awake, there's no guarantee she'll be mentally present. She might not recognize me. She might be experiencing an aggressive, hallucinatory episode. She

might scream when I walk into the room. The nurse
might ask me to leave. Like last time.

I clench my jaw, weighing the sickening
pros and cons.

Eight hours. Eight hours. One-third of my final day.
Bare minimum. Probably more.

It's a brutal choice, but ultimately I decide ... no. I'm
not flying to California. This conversation with mom
was as perfect as I could hope for. She was present. She
was feisty. She was ... herself. I love her, and I want my
final memory of her to be positive and comforting, not
an agonized race against the clock.

I got to say "I love you" one last time. I'm
grateful for that.

Grateful ... but also nauseated.

*It's not fair. It's not fair. Stay here or fly to see her, there's
no option that feels completely right. I'm a terrible daughter.
I should go. I shouldn't go. I don't have enough time. I might
have just enough time. I feel sick.*

Full-length thoughts shatter into fragments.

I can't. I hate. I can't. I ... I ...

An energy surges through my body, like I've never
felt before. It's grief. It's rage. It's an emotion that doesn't
even have a word, at least not in the English language.
Animalistic. Beyond description. I smash the corded
phone into the metal sheathing of the booth until my

knuckles are raw, oozing, and coated with flecks of blue and silver paint.

I sob until I've wrenched every last drop of saline from my body, tears flooding my shirt, and there's nothing more that I can give.

Hour Six

I head back into the burger restaurant because I don't know where else to go.

I rinse my raw knuckles in the bathroom sink. The waitress seems nonplussed when I reenter and even motions for me to return to my previous booth, which is empty. Her expression reads, *"If you want it, it's all yours."*

I'm grateful for a quiet place to sit and collect myself. I order a black coffee with sugar. There's a copy of last week's *City Pages* sitting near my booth—one of those free, weekly independent newspapers filled with horoscopes and classifieds and op-ed pieces on why the state government really needs to stop putzing around and reduce public-school classroom sizes already. I leaf through the pages, not looking for anything in particular, just hungry for a temporary reprieve from my own mind. Because if I really allow myself to feel everything I am feeling, I'm pretty sure I will scream. Or vomit. Or head back out to the phone booth and reduce it to rubble.

I take a deep breath and then sip the sweet, inky coffee. On the back cover of the paper is the usual smattering of classified ads and earnest invitations to join market research focus groups and medical testing programs (*"Got herpes? Apply now!"*). One ad catches my eye. An illustration of a lily flower swoops over the text.

You've invested in TCR. Now plan your fabulous farewell. It's your final day. Do it your way! Email Tasha to schedule your complimentary consultation.

I read the text several times over. "Your fabulous farewell"? That's the euphemism to end all euphemisms. Could this "Tasha" be some kind of event planner, except for Temporary Cellular Resuscitation? It makes sense in a morbid kind of way. I mean, people plan elaborate parties for birthdays, anniversaries, baptisms, and bar mitzvahs. Why not hire an event planner to expertly coordinate your final day on earth?

Overcome with curiosity, I drop a five-dollar bill on the table—more than enough to cover my cup of coffee, I figure—and I tear off the corner of the paper with Tasha's phone number and address.

Back inside the pay phone, I curse as I realize that I punched and slammed the dial tone right out of the phone. It's broken. A feeble *blleeeezt* is all that emits from the earpiece before spluttering and going silent.

I curse myself again for hastily tossing my iPhone in the garbage can back at the hospital. Without any way to call or text, I feel oddly naked—like one of those "going to work without your clothes on" dreams where you suddenly realize that your coworkers are staring at your bare nipples, and you're vulnerable, stupid, and alone.

I stare at the shred of newspaper again. Well, she's got an address and it's a weekday. She's probably at her office. Why not pay Tasha a visit in person? I have no other plans. And I have literally nothing to lose.

Hour Seven

Tasha's office is not far. I walk briskly—nothing like imminent death to put a spring in your step—until the street curves around, bringing me to face a nondescript warehouse-style building right by the railroad tracks.

It looks abandoned and forlorn until you get up close. Some enterprising architect-designer-type has gutted the interior and replaced it with a gleaming, modern aesthetic. Total renovation. Polished concrete floors, probably retained from the original warehouse, but glossed and spiffed up. Exposed brick walls. Rose-gold chandeliers adding a touch of femininity to the otherwise stark, hard-edged space. It's all visible from the sidewalk through a series of glass panels that reach from floor to ceiling. A placard by the entrance displays about a dozen business names.

001 Red Fox Graphic Design

002 Studio VI Personal Training

003 Your Fabulous Farewell – Tasha Lockwood

I stop there. Yep. That's her.

I buzz in and a perky voice greets me almost immediately.

"Yes? Hello?"

"Um, hi, I'm looking for Tasha Lockwood? I don't have an appointment, but . . ." *Bzzzzt.*

Apparently walk-in clients are welcome here.

I step inside the warehouse, and I'm greeted by a sultry vanilla fragrance that seems to be emanating from every corner of the space—as if perfume is routinely pumped through the air-conditioning vents. It's a pleasant touch, albeit unexpected.

I seem to be in some type of waiting lounge. The lighting is rosy and flattering. Sleek couches and ottomans are tucked into each corner in little groupings of twos and threes. I can imagine hip young entrepreneurs gathering here to talk about search engine optimization and social media-driven marketing and viral crowd-funding or whatever the buzzword of the week may be.

The space is oddly empty, but then ...

Whoa.

Tasha, I can only presume, comes striding towards me in all her glory.

She's well over six feet tall in her staggeringly high heels, and she's clad in a Pepto Bismol-pink dress that looks like a cross between the world's softest leather and liquid latex, with a plunging neckline displaying a generous pair of breasts. Her legs reach from here until eternity. Her lavender-colored hair is chopped into an asymmetrical bob.

She looks like a cross between Betty Boop and a pixie fairy creature from outer space. As she nears me, I notice pink and purple glitter cascading across her collarbones. Because why not, right?

Before we've exchanged a single word, she pulls me in for a tight, full-body hug that lasts, oh, just a little bit too long for most people's comfort. She smells like ripe strawberries and ... I can't help myself. A rush of grief washes through me—grief for my father's lost battle with cancer, for my mother's slow dirge-crawl into senility, for my own death just hours before, for the supreme over-ness of it all—and I cry. My tears fall, hot, hard, and sloppy, creating rivulets of glitter on her shoulders.

She holds me closer as if this is fine, normal, expected, not a problem.

She makes comforting sounds, shushing and nodding, the way a mother might comfort a hysterical child.

My sobs echo in the empty entrance hall. One minute. Two. I can't seem to stop, but then suddenly, I am done. Depleted. After I've emptied myself fully, I feel exhausted, like a child who has cried herself to sleep.

I silently pray this is the last time I burst into tears today. Jesus Christ. Enough already.

Tasha peels her latex-encased breasts away from my chest. She smiles kindly, long lashes framing a pair of lavender eyes that match her pastel-alien hair.

"Better?" she asks. I nod.

She grabs my hand like we're BFFs skipping towards Mr. Johnson's "Intro to American History" class in seventh grade and tugs me towards her office.

"Come on," she says. "Let's plan your farewell."

Hour Eight

I sink into a tufted chair encased in silver crushed velvet with gold tassels. I get the impression that when it comes to clothing and makeup and furniture and pretty much everything else, Tasha's personal motto is: *"But why stop there?"*

"Do you have an approximate sense of when you are going to pass on? Do you have a terminal illness? A life expectancy estimation from your doctor, or . . ." she gives me a no-judgment glance, ". . . will you be determining the final date on your own?"

Tasha eyes me expectantly with an expression of absolute warmth and understanding. I get the feeling she's impossible to shock. I also get the feeling that most of her clients probably have the foresight to contact her, uh, before they are already dead.

I fidget nervously. Maybe I'm wasting her time—and mine. Maybe it's too late for me.

"Um, so . . ." My fingers wander across the arm of the chair. ". . . It's already happening. I mean, they already, um, I already . . ."

Tasha's eyes widen, but she retains her composure. Such a pro.

"So you are, ah, I see. You are already . . ."

"Dead," I finish bluntly. We lock eyes as the D-word reverberates from my lips.

"I'm doing my 'bonus round' right now. I'm about eight hours in, which means I have about sixteen to go."

She removes a fresh notebook from a desk drawer and begins to take notes with a hot pink pen. Something about her unflappable composure makes me feel like I can confess anything to her. And the fact that she's a complete stranger makes it easier. She's like a priest. A bubblegum pink priest with three-inch-wide heart-shaped earrings.

I find myself gushing and babbling as if I'm right inside a confessional booth.

"So, like, I woke up. I walked outside the hospital. I saw this couple in love, kissing in front of the hospital, and I just lost it. I felt so lonely. I mean, seriously, so lonely it actually hurt. Then I had a cheeseburger. Then I called my mom. Then I found your ad in the paper. And now here I am."

I'm talking quickly, almost panting for breath. Her face is absolutely serene and inviting—so I continue.

"I want to do something to make this day mean something, you know? I want it to matter. I don't want it to just slip away. But I don't know what I'm doing. I don't know the 'right' way to spend this time. I mean, this is it. Like *really it*. I need this day to mean something. I need … I need what's left of my life to mean something."

I feel tears prickling yet again, and she hands me a Kleenex, withdrawn deftly from some invisible compartment of her desk.

"Can you help me?" I finish, softly. "I mean … is it too late? Can you plan a, um, special day for someone like me? Someone who is already gone?"

Tasha says nothing. Her eyes look glassy, as if she, too, is fighting back tears.

She stands—remarkably steady in shimmering purple-and-gold platform heels that a drag queen might deem "a bit over the top"—and she swings over to a compartment in the corner of her office. She withdraws a tall, slim bottle filled with a pale turquoise liquor and pours two champagne flutes halfway full. She tops them off with sparkling wine, arranges both glasses on a silver tray, and returns to the desk. Still not a word.

Arranging herself in her seat, she nods towards the drinks, picks up one of the flutes, and raises a glass towards me. I pick up the other one, mirroring her movements. Bubbles rise like mermaid kisses from the base to the top, fizzing into nothingness.

Tasha tilts her glass towards mine.

Clink.

She downs her drink in one go and I follow suit. Warmth floods my body, my anxiety lifts, and I have

the subtlest sense of time slowing down. Like lying
on your back and staring at clouds that move almost
imperceptibly across the sky, so slow, it's like it's not
even happening. I wonder what was in that drink. Then I
decide: I don't care.

She sets her empty glass down on the table and
reaches across to clasp my hands. Her eyes shine
with determination.

"What is your name?" she asks, still holding my
hands firmly.

"Nora," I reply.

She nods, giving my hands a gentle squeeze.

"Well, Nora … I have some very good news for you."

"What?"

"Today is not over yet."

Hour Nine

"Since time is of the essence, we're going to shorten my standard client intake process."

Tasha produces a pair of lavender-rimmed reading glasses seemingly out of thin air.

Her cheeks are flushed from the drink—or possibly sheer elation. I can tell: this is a woman who genuinely loves her work.

"How long have you been doing this?" I ask, curious. "I mean, planning 'farewell days' or whatever you call it?"

Her cheeks flush a deep shade of rose. She gives me a small smile that can only be described as "adorably sheepish."

"Actually, ah ... I opened my business last week," she confesses. "You are my very first client." Her tone quickens. "But prior to doing this work, I was the creative director for the top wedding and event planning agency in the city. Before that I majored in hospitality with a minor in sociology. And in high school I was president of the ..."

"Stop, stop!" I giggle. "You don't have to sell me on your credentials. It's OK. You're hired. Besides, it's not like I've got tons of time to shop around, right?"

I make a pathetic attempt at a wink, which probably just looks like a facial convulsion. I've always been severely wink-challenged.

She gives me a gracious "thank you" grin and winks back. Perfectly, of course.

"Speaking of 'hired' . . ." I continue. "What do you charge for your services?"

She shakes her head dramatically.

"No charge. Like I said, you're my very first client. Let me design your final day. It will be invaluable training for me. Truly, it would be my privilege."

I ponder her offer, feeling slightly uneasy. I'm one of those weird people who likes paying full price for people's services. I never like feeling like I'm taking advantage of anyone. But she seems completely assured in her decision. OK. Fine. I'm in.

"Deal," I say. "But let me at least write a testimonial for your website or Yelp or whatever." She laughs, and we shake on it.

"OK! Let's get back to those intake forms. Just a few questions here. Full name?"

"Nora Hamilton."

"Any relation to Alexander?"

"Nope. I wish."

She smiles, pushing her glasses back onto the bridge of her nose. "Next question," she continues. "Age?"

"Thirty-two."

"Occupation?"

I heave a sigh.

"Uh, can we skip that one?" I attempt a light-hearted tone, but I can't mask the heaviness beneath the words. "The truth is that I never really figured out what my 'calling' was supposed to be. Sad, right?"

She peeks up from her notepad, pen poised in hand.

"Not sad. What are some jobs you've held in the past?"

I exhale sullenly. This is a touchy topic for me. I'm a chronic flip-flopper when it comes to my career. My résumé looks like a computer program randomized a bunch of bizarre job titles and slapped them together on a piece of paper. It's a hot mess.

"Jobs I've had? Um. Let's see. Lifeguard. Library assistant. Blogger, if that counts. I managed a coffee shop for a while. Then I worked at a specialty health food store that sold gluten-free pancake mixes and stuff, which was hilarious because I'm like, obsessed with bread. Um, then I worked as a hostess at a fancy French restaurant. Then I tried to write a novel … but that didn't really go anywhere. After that, I went back to hostessing and waitressing because at least I could make decent money doing that," I cringe. "God. This is pathetic, right?"

I notice that Tasha stopped taking notes somewhere between "blogger" and "pancake." She flips to a fresh page in her notebook and tries a different tactic.

"Can you remember the last time someone gave you a compliment that meant a lot to you? What did they say?" she asks.

No one's ever asked me that before. I roll back through a few recent memories. Nothing seems to leap out. But then ... hmm, yeah. Maybe that.

"So this was a long time ago, back when I was working in the coffee shop," I begin. Her pen starts moving again.

"I used to draw little cartoons on the customers' coffee cups. Nothing that amazing or anything. Just little doodles. People's faces. Their kids. The dogs they would bring by. Or little details that I had learned about their lives. Sometimes I would write a little message, like inspiring quotes or whatever. I just did it because it was fun and because I knew it made people happy. Something to pass the time during slow shifts. . . ."

"One day, a regular came by. I handed over her usual coffee—with a cute doodle of her dog Sandy on the cup in black Sharpie—and before she left the shop, she told me something that kinda surprised me."

Tasha leans forward, eyebrows sky-high, with a look that practically screams, *"Whaaat???"*

"This woman told me that she had kept almost every coffee cup I had ever given her. Dozens of cups with my drawings on each of them. She told me she used a hole puncher and threaded some yarn through all of the empty cups, like a string of paper lanterns, and she put them up inside her cubicle at work. She told me those drawings always made her smile. She wanted to tell me how much she appreciated my doodles and how I always brightened her day. I literally could not believe it. I mean, I'm not even that good at drawing . . ."

Tasha's pen comes to a halt. She listens intently to my story as if it's the most fascinating thing she's heard in her entire life. My words trail off awkwardly. I glance up to meet her gaze.

"Nora," she says. "I have a suspicion about you."

"What's that?"

She smiles knowingly.

"You are a daymaker."

"A what?"

"Daymaker," she repeats. "Haven't you heard that term before? It's a term that a man named David Wagner came up with. He's an entrepreneur here in Minneapolis. He's one of my personal heroes, actually. It means that when someone comes into your life, you 'make their day.' You don't even have to try that hard. You can't help it. It's just who you are. You are thoughtful and caring and creative, and you want people to be happy."

She continues:

"I bet with every single job you've had, you were
the brightest spark in everyone's day. I bet every single
manager hated to see you go and begged you to stay.
I bet customers arranged their schedules so that they
would make sure to swing by during *your* shift. I bet
that woman wasn't the only customer who loved every
coffee cup drawing that you did. I bet you touched many
people's lives. More than you realize."

"Daymaker," I repeat back. I like the sound of that.
And weirdly enough, I think she's right.

My work history might be scattered and eclectic—
compared to some people's, I guess—but I've always
made it my personal mission to leave other people in
better condition than I found them. I know how to make
customers feel special and appreciated. I can always
make my coworkers crack a smile, even the jaded ones
who are just trudging along towards retirement. Even
back when I worked as a lifeguard at a summer camp,
over a decade ago, I always went above and beyond the
call of duty. I always made an effort to talk to the shy
kids who were afraid of the deep end so they wouldn't
feel so alone. It's true. I love making people's days better.
I always have.

Damn.

Maybe my life wasn't just a scattered waste, a trail of
career indecision.

Maybe I did make a difference in a few people's lives.

"Jesus, Tasha . . ." I say, feeling all the loose, ragged ends of my story knit neatly together. "You just changed my entire opinion of myself. What you said ... it just means a lot to me. Thank you. So much."

"Shall we toast to that?" she giggles, already rising to fix us another round of cocktails.

"Yeah. Let's."

We clink glasses again, sipping our champagne-infused drinks a bit more slowly this time, savoring each sparkle and bubble.

"Next question," she continues. "What is something you've always wanted to do that you never got around to? Something you were always saving for 'someday' in the future?"

"What, you mean like, skydiving?"

"Is skydiving something you've always wanted to do?" The tone in her voice reads, *"Because we can make than happen. I know people. With parachutes."*

"Not particularly," I reply.

"So what then? Any guilty pleasures ... secret dreams . . . ?"

I take another sip of my drink, feeling incredibly boring because of what I am about to confess.

"Um, this is probably totally lame, but . . ."

Tasha's eyes are gleaming. She's unconsciously pressing herself over the desk, inching closer to me. I can tell she *lives* for this. I continue.

". . . I have always been curious about online dating."

"Curious? Like, you mean, curious to try it?"

"Yeah," I say. "I mean, I know that tons of people are doing it, and it's not that special or unusual these days, but for whatever reason, I never gave it a shot. I always thought about it but never did it. Just nervous, I guess."

"What is it about online dating that appeals to you?" she asks.

My mind drifts back to my childhood home. A two-bedroom apartment near Elliot Park. Hardwood floors that needed a good polishing, but never got one. Glass-paned windows with copper locks that frosted over during the wintertime and fogged up with heat during the summer. Mom and dad slow dancing to Puccini, laughing, whispering, kissing, and sneaking a quick ass-squeeze while pasta simmers on the stove. I'm hiding under the table, a little too young to understand what makes this scene so compelling, but I am awestruck nonetheless. I can't take my eyes away. It's true love. I know it.

My mind sifts through fragmented stories, floating back to the legendary story of how my parents first met. It was a party thrown by a mutual acquaintance. Neither of them had intended to attend. Except they did. A last-minute choice. A chance meeting. The chemistry was instant, they never parted, and the rest was history.

I've never experienced a love like they shared. It's something I always yearned for. Beneath my slight tendency towards sarcasm and the fierce independence that I inherited from my mom, the truth is, I'm a total softie marshmallow mush-pile and a hopeless romantic. It's just I never got the chance to experience deep, crazy, Nicholas Sparks-level love. I searched. I tried. I just never found it. Nothing even close.

"Online dating?" Tasha pipes up again, waiting for my response. "Why is it something you want to try?"

I blurt out my response.

"Because I think my soul mate is out there somewhere. And maybe he wants to meet me. Badly. Just as badly as I want to meet him."

"Nora, are you aware that you *literally* started glowing just now? Your face, your skin, everything. You're radiant. This needs to happen. WE ARE MAKING THIS HAPPEN!"

She's not actually screaming at me, but the intensity of her voice is bordering on "five alarm fire emergency."

"What, you mean like … make an online dating profile? For me? Right now??"

"YESSSS!"

OK, *now* she's screaming at me. But it's a loving, supportive kind of scream.

Before I have time to register what is happening, she has pulled up an array of different dating websites in various tabs on her iPad.

"Any preference?" she asks, clicking swiftly through each tab. "Tinder? Bumble? OKCupid? Lather? Frackle? Matchee?"

I wave my hands dismissively. Don't care. Whatever.

"I'll choose one then," she announces. Before I have time to blink—or protest—she's snapping photos of me with the camera on her tablet.

"For your profile!" she explains mid-snap.

Embarrassed, I glance down at my hands. I hear the shutter-clicks come to a stop.

Finally. Relieved, I look up with a smile.

CLICK.

One last guerilla shot.

"That's the one!" she cries, flipping the screen around to show me.

I grimace, bracing myself. I've never been entirely stoked about how I look in photos. But maybe she's a photographic genius, or maybe she just caught me at the right moment, because this time, I am pleasantly surprised.

I lean closer towards the photo on her screen. My skin looks soft and smooth, dotted with freckles across my cheekbones. My smile is warm and relaxed, showing just a hint of the small gap between my front teeth—the one that everybody except my mom and dad encouraged me to get "fixed." My dark hair is half-covering part of my cheek, falling in curls down my shoulders and back.

"Gorgeous," Tasha declares, and I have to agree. Not half bad.

With staggering speed, she fills out a profile for me—presumably drawing upon details from our "client intake" chat, bolstered by her own imagination. I lean back, savoring the rest of my drink, letting her work her magic.

"One last section. Favorite food, favorite book, sexual orientation." Easy enough.

"Burgers, *The Magicians*, straight … ish," I clarify.

"Favorite quote?"

"We are all in the gutter, but some of us are looking at the stars."

"Which was said by … ?"

"Oscar Wilde."

"Perfection," she coos, flipping the tablet around once again, handing it to me.

I skim through the profile that she's whipped together. It's simple. Bare bones. Not too much information. Just the basics. My smiling, freckled, slightly gap-toothed face grins back at me. I shrug.

"Good enough, I guess?"

Ping.

A digital note fills the room, and Tasha grabs
the tablet from my hands with the enthusiasm of a
velociraptor tearing into a fresh New York strip steak.

"OMG!!!!!!" she squeals. "You already got a star.
Not just gold. A PLATINUM star!" She's practically
trembling with excitement. I can't help but get swept up
into her tizzy.

"That means he really likes you. OH my GOD.
He's cute. And he's online right now. Should we
message him?"

I shrug again, getting the feeling that "no" is a
response that will not be tolerated.

"We're messaging him," she agrees with ... herself.

"Hey there . . ." she dictates aloud, typing into the
tablet, eyeing me for approval. "Thanks for the platinum
star. You're crazy hot."

"Stop right there," I intervene. "I would never
say that."

"What?"

"Crazy hot."

"OK, well, what would you say?"

I tug the tablet out of her hands and gaze at this
mysterious platinum-star-doling gentleman. I do my
best not to gawk. Because she's right. He's ... crazy hot.
Like "hottt," triple-t hot.

He's tall, not bulkily muscled, but toned, with jet
black hair knotted into a bun on the top of his head.

Shaved on the sides. A vibrant tattoo curls up the side of his neck, giving him a punky samurai vibe.

In one profile photo, he's wearing a crisp white uniform, and he appears to be teaching kids how to karate-chop a wooden block into two chunks. The kids are gazing at him with obvious adoration. Some kind of martial arts instructor, maybe? He's definitely fit and athletic. But what really grips me are his eyes. Dark hazel-honey-colored eyes, fringed with unfairly long lashes. I could fall into those eyes and keep falling forever. . . .

I realize my jaw is hanging open ever-so-slightly. I look up at Tasha, and she's staring at me with a *"told you so ... "* smirk.

I skim through the non-photography portion of his profile.

Apparently, he loves listening to The Chainsmokers (me too), Chopin (unexpected choice, very cool) and reading "the latest article on Vice.com and also poetry by Rumi and Hafiz."

"Sooo?" Tasha breaks my reverie. "You have GOT to send a message to him. What are you going to write?"

Maybe it's the fact that I'm already two cocktails deep, or the fact that I have absolutely nothing to lose, but I instantly know what my approach is going to be.

From memory, I type a short poem directly into the message field. It's a poem about a mystical game of tag where God says, "Tag, you're it!" and wonderful things transpire. "Major-league wonderful," the poet says. It's one of my favorites.

I hit "send" and hand the tablet back to Tasha.

She skims through my note and gives me a *"WTF?"* expression.

"It's a poem. A pretty famous one. He'll recognize it … I think," I respond.

She smiles kindly, flicking through a few more profiles, checking to see if I have any other potential matches.

Ping.

She taps the screen and says nothing, biting back emotion. She turns the screen to me. AikidoGuy82 has responded to my message. Already.

Thirty-three words that thrill me, sending tendrils of heat up my spine.

> Hey. I love that poem. I'm off work in 30 minutes. I know this is super spontaneous, but I'm actually free this afternoon. Want to meet up? Let me know. Tag you're it.

I glance at Tasha and she nods empathically. *YES.*
I type back.
OK, sure!

And then, because it's one of my favorite places in town, I add, Let's meet by the cherry-spoon at the Walker Sculpture Garden. I click SEND and hold my breath.

His reply comes instantly.

See you there.

Hour Ten

"MAKEOVER!!!!" Tasha squeals, with the eardrum-shattering decibel level of a rocket breaking through the sound barrier.

"You're kidding, right?"

"Uh, NO I am not kidding. This might be the last date of your entire life—no offense—and you are going to look one thousand percent boner-rific."

I glance at my gray cotton cargo pants and baggy white T-shirt—the clothes they doled out to me at the hospital. Barely one step up from hospital scrubs.

"Not boner-rific enough?" I ask in mock astonishment.

"Nora, you'd look hot wearing a filthy burlap sack . . ." she says, grinning, "But why not pull out all the stops? How much time until your date?"

"About thirty minutes. Not much time."

She blows out her cheeks, sighing with irritation. I get the sense that her typical morning routine begins at 4 a.m. with a deep conditioning hair masque and concludes with a double set of false eyelashes at a quarter to noon.

"Not ideal, but that will have to do. Let's get started."

Twenty minutes later, my hair has been styled into soft mermaid waves, my eyelids have been lined with charcoal-black liner and dusted with shimmery powder, my lips have been glossed with some kind of coconut-scented situation, and my body has been arranged into a soft dress with a scooping back and deep pockets in the front. I like the pockets most of all. Somewhere to hide my nervous hands.

Tasha doesn't have a bra that fits me, so I go without, which is my preference anyway. She whips through a couple of scarves, bags, and accessories from a hidden closet that has basically dropped from the wall like one of those magical fold-out Murphy beds.

"Shoe size?"

"Eight," I reply.

She tosses me a pair of leather sandals. Flat and very chic. Navy blue silk ties wrap around the ankles. They're very summery and surprisingly comfortable.

"My sister works for a clothing and shoe designer in Manhattan," she says, by way of explanation. "She ships me a truckload of free stuff every season."

"Wow."

She shoots me a look that says, *"I know. I would murder without remorse for that kind of workplace perk."*

"OK!" she says, taking a few steps back to appraise me. "Twirl."

I comply, fanning my arms out for dramatic effect, like a jubilant woman in a Tampon commercial who has just discovered that, YES, she CAN play volleyball on the beach in a string bikini without having to worry about a goddamn thing.

Tasha giggles.

"Nora, you look . . ." she dabs her eyes, and I wish she'd stop, because I'm teetering on the edge of another emotional meltdown myself. I'm swinging between elation and despair. This day is the biggest rollercoaster. "You look ... you look so ALIVE."

I smile weakly. I can feel the tears coming. Goddamn it. Again?

She senses it, too.

"No no noooo!" she half-sobs, half-laughs, lunging for the box of Kleenex. "I worked too hard on that smoky eye. No tears. Cut it out."

We both collapse into giggles, and for a moment, our souls are transported back to another time—another lifetime, maybe. It's summertime, and we're bunkmates at camp, play-fighting over who gets to keep the "BE FRI" half of the heart necklace and who gets "ST ENDS."

Our eyes lock. I wonder if she feels this multiple-lifetimes-of-connection-forever sensation too, or if it's just a one-sided delusion. She smiles again. I think she feels it, too. I'm choosing to believe it's true.

"I should get going," I say.

"Already called you an Uber," she responds, tapping her phone. "And ... your driver is here. Downstairs, waiting by the curb. Get going. Have fun!"

"But, wait, how will I ... I mean, afterwards, what about . . ."

Tasha shushes me out the door.

"HAVE FUN," she says insistently. "This is your post-dying wish, right? Online date? With a hot stranger? A true love connection, possibly? Who knows what might happen? Tell me everything afterwards. Or don't ... and just die in his arms tonight."

"Not funny," I scowl.

She places both hands on my shoulders, giving me one final nudge towards the door.

"Daymaker, Nora. Daymaker. Remember who you are. Have fun. Make his day, but more importantly, make yours. This is your time. Do all the things. Feel all the feelings. Enjoy yourself to the max. And remember that you are amazing. This guy is lucky to spend twenty seconds in your presence."

"Daymaker," I repeat to myself. "Right. OK. I'll just, uh, go ... blow his mind? I guess?"

"Or MORE than that!" she cackles.

I scurry back through the waiting area, looking back over my shoulder for a moment, casting one more glance at Tasha's peony-pink lips and tousled lavender hair, wondering if I will ever see my new BFF again.

Before I can procrastinate any longer, the Uber driver steps out of the black sedan that's idling at the curb. He opens the rear passenger side door for me, smiling politely.

This is really happening.

My first date in nearly two years.

On the last day of my life.

Hour Eleven

The cherry-spoon rises in front of me—massive, bizarre, unlike any sculpture on earth.

It's literally a gigantic silver spoon, hundreds of feet tall, swooping from the depths of a serene pond towards the cotton-candy-blue sky. Balanced precariously in the center of the spoon is a rich, seductive, gleaming cherry. I've heard they polish the cherry once per year to maintain its otherworldly shine.

It's peculiar and beautiful, nestled here in the center of a fairly ordinary public park.

Taking in the view, I feel a pang of regret.

The Walker Sculpture Garden is one of my favorite places in Minneapolis—a place I should have visited a lot more often. Really, I should have visited every single weekend—instead of working or watching Netflix or Facebooking or whatever seemed more important at the time. I should have eaten lunch here every day. I should have walked through the garden with my dad more often back when he was alive. I should have . . .

I shake off the fog of regret. I'm here now. That's what counts.

The cherry-spoon is an unmistakable landmark, so there's no possible chance that AikidoGuy82 could miss me. Unless, of course, he doesn't recognize me from my photo. But he will. I think. In any event, I have no doubt that I will recognize him.

I am phone-less, watch-less, clock-less, and witless with pre-date jitters. I figure it's getting close to our appointed meeting time. But maybe not. Am I early? Too late? Maybe he looked for me and I wasn't there yet? Did I miss my chance?

I feel compelled to lunge at a passing family to inquire about the time. The mother is cooing at her infant in the stroller. I decide not to pester them.

Instead, I lie down in the grass, ankles crossed, arms folded behind my head, enjoying the soft spray of the fountain at the base of the cherry-spoon sculpture.

I allow my eyes to close, noticing the way my other senses ignite in the absence of sight. The percolation of the fountain. The soft misting of the water prickling my thighs. Distant laughter. The instructional tone of a teacher, or tour guide leader, guiding a flock of visitors through the park. The throbbing heat of the mid-afternoon sun on my face.

Just a little too warm. The kind that makes you crave deep shade and an ice cube slithering down the back of your dress.

Keeping my eyes closed, I extend my arms above my head, feeling the grass tickle my shoulder blades as I stretch, fully, deeply, from head to toe, like when you first wake up in the morning. I arch my back slightly, luxuriating in the sunlight, wondering, somewhat morbidly, if this is what it feels like on the other side. Dark. No sight. Yet, somehow, infinitely delicious.

"Wow and ... hi," It's a masculine voice, summoning me from my reverie. "Is that you?"

I gaze upwards. Blazing sunlight smacks my face, half-blinding me, casting the figure in a shapeless black-gold halo. Squinting, I roll onto all fours, and he kneels down to my level in one fluid motion, graceful as a dancer. Our eyes meet. Deep green and molten hazel. He is unfairly, almost painfully attractive. I resist the urge to gasp and swoon like a girl in a cheesy romance novel. But I want to.

"Are you ... AikidoGuy82?" I ask.

He smiles, and his teeth are not perfect. Slightly crooked with the subtlest hint of an underbite. Somehow, this only makes him even more deliriously attractive.

"Renzo," he says. "But everybody calls me Ren. Great to meet you. And you are ... ?"

I nod dumbly, not quite comprehending the English language. After a beat, he tries again.

"What's your name?"

Oh, right. He asked me that already, and I forgot to answer because his eyes have dissolved my brain into waffle batter.

"Nora," I respond, legitimately proud of myself for forming words with my mouth.

"Nora. That's so pretty." Hearing him say my name and the phrase "so pretty" in the same sentence almost drives me into unconsciousness. Jesus Christ. I've emotionally regressed into a fifteen-year-old girl at a Justin Bieber concert.

"So ... are we doing the kneeling-crouching thing for a while?" he asks, gesturing at the grass beneath my fingers and knees. "I mean, I have zero complaints if that's the case . . ."

I smile. There's a hint of mischief in his voice. Just the right amount of flirtatious.

I make my way to my feet, and he follows, gliding gracefully, like someone who's masterfully in command of every muscle and tendon in his body. He rises about seven inches above me. My cheeks would nestle perfectly into that warm spot where chest melts into shoulder.

"This might be weird, but . . ." "Uh oh," he smirks. "Weirdness? Already? Aren't you supposed to date me for at least six weeks before the weirdness begins?" He crosses his arms in mock frustration. "Lay it on me."

". . . Can I give you a hug?"

His face softens. The smirky, cool-guy persona dissolves. Suddenly, he's just a human being in a T-shirt and jeans, standing in front of a woman who desperately wants to press her body into his, which is, perhaps, a slightly odd request given that we've just met, and yet both of our eyes are pleading for connection, and so I hope he'll say . . .

"Yeah, sure."

Stepping forward, he closes the small strip of space between us. A cloud passes across the sun, creating a momentary wisp of shade.

"Come here."

He wraps me in his arms. Mine encircle his waist. We fit. It's effortless. Seamless. Soothing and stimulating all at once. It feels like sipping warm coffee from a thermos while the sun rises over the ocean.

"Whoa," I exhale softly.

I don't even mean to say anything, but it slips out, and I know he hears me because he tugs me a little closer. We stay like that, woven together, hearts beating against skin wrapped in thin layers of fabric. Like mourners comforting each other at funeral. Like lovers waltzing at a wedding. Like friends reuniting after decades apart. Like everything.

Minutes pass. Children scamper into the fountain at the base of the cherry-spoon sculpture, desperate to cool off while their parents bark various commands. *"Get back." "Not there." "Time to go."* Another tour group ambles by. Knitted closely, we remain still.

I rest my cheek against that perfectly sculptured part of his chest, the part that seems custom-contoured for the shape of my face.

A few more minutes pass. Not a single one wasted. There is nowhere else I'd rather be, nothing else I'd rather be doing. This moment feels like coming home. It's ludicrous, but it's true. I wonder if he feels it, too.

I peel my cheek away from his sea salt-scented body and tilt my eyes upwards. He waits for me to speak.

What I want to do is say something impossibly cool. Something simple and precise. The perfectly choreographed words of a character from an Emmy Award-winning TV show. Instead, my words come out in a rapid tumble of need, desire, hunger, and awkwardness.

"So ... hi Ren. OK. Here's the deal. I'm only here for a little while. I know this might sound rushed or whatever, but I want to skip the formalities and just ... be with you. Like, let's skip the part where we have a chit-chatty conversation over dinner, and pay twelve dollars to see a movie that we don't even want to see, and then wait three days to text each other, and then send emojis back and forth and try to interpret what everything means, and all of that typical dating stuff. Let's just ... be together. Spend time together. In real life. Right here. Right now. Are you into that?"

If he's stunned by my outpouring, he doesn't show it.

"So, you quote poetry by Hafiz, you're not interested in small talk or shitty movies, and you're only in town for a little while . . ." he summarizes.

"Something like that."

". . . and you're breathtakingly beautiful, and you want to spend time with me."

At "beautiful," my heart supernova-explodes into ten thousand fragments of excitement.

"Correct."

He pulls me back into a hug. This time, curling his fingers through my hair, sending shivers up my spine and then downward, to each of my toes.

"Yeah, Nora. I'm into that."

I exhale deeply. Relieved. Exhilarated. Slightly guilty, too, for lying to him about only being "here for a little while." Except it's not exactly a lie. It's true. Well, true-ish.

The pheromone haze of his body distracts me from my inner ramblings. He gently cups the back of my head with one hand, stroking my shoulders and spine with the other.

"So, Nora, what kind of afternoon did you have in mind?"

I blush from head to toe. (Dear Tasha Lockwood: wherever you are, please accept this telepathic text message: *THANK YOU*.)

"Do you have a car?" I ask.

"Yeah. Don't get too excited, though. 2002 VW Rabbit. It runs great except for when it doesn't."

The park is quickly filling with couples and families and assorted pedestrians. Must be close to 5 p.m. The post-workday flood of humanity. I want to get out here and be alone with Ren. Somewhere quieter.

"Take me to your car, drive me somewhere amazing, and make out with me," I instruct boldly, feeling surprised at my uncharacteristically bossy tone. Did that seriously just come out of my mouth? Apparently it did. And judging by his expression, he's not offended by the suggestion.

I start marching in the direction of the park exit. He strides quickly behind, catching up with me easily. His clasps my hand and pulls me close.

"How do you know I'm not an axe murderer with sinister plans for you?" he asks with a comedic glint in his eye.

I giggle. Wouldn't that be a hilarious twist.

"I could ask you the same thing . . ." I retort. "You don't know me at all."

He doesn't know me. And vice versa. Typically, that would concern me. But somehow, today, it doesn't matter.

I don't know if this feeling will last, but right now, inside of this moment, I am completely unburdened. There is no more guilt about the past. No anxiety about the future. No schedule. No agenda. No obligations that need to be fulfilled. Just me and this beautiful man who is willing to spend a few hours of his life by my side.

I slip into the passenger seat of his car. He pulls into reverse, and I study the sculpted shape of his forearm with fascination, drinking in every detail.

There's a faded Jansport backpack in the backseat, a pair of sneakers that smell like well-used sneakers do, a folded karate uniform—it's called a *gi*, I think—a half-empty water bottle and then, down by my feet in the front, one peanut butter-flavored protein bar wrapper. The interior of his car is not messy, exactly, but it's not tidy either. It's boyish and human and I love it.

I roll down my window and he mirrors me. He flashes me a smile and I die. No. Actually, the opposite. I live.

Hour Twelve

I hear the falls before I see them.

A symphonic roar of water, crashing and pounding, swallowing all other sounds.

Gravel crunches beneath my sandaled feet as we move closer to the edge of the water. Late afternoon sunlight, soft and dappled, weaves through tree tops and pours onto the trail. The world is green and honey-gold, and the air is layered with sweetness: clean grass laced with flower blossoms, the faintest trace of warm, freshly-pressed waffle cones from the ice cream stand back in the parking lot.

With each step down the trail, the thundering of the falls grows louder, and the rest of the world fades away. The chattering families and stroller-pushing parents have long since peeled away from the path. There's nobody here. Only us.

I can see the white column of water cascading on the rocks, just off in the distance. We're close enough to feel the spray on our skin.

Minnehaha Falls.

Yet another local landmark I promised myself I'd visit more often, one of these days, except I never seemed to make the time. For the dozenth time today, I remind myself, *"I'm here now. That's what matters."*

Ren laughs as I kick off my sandals and dip one toe into the cool water.

He stops laughing when I peel off my white sundress, revealing absolutely nothing underneath. It's probably the boldest thing I've done in my entire life—and while it's a vaguely creepy and inappropriate thought, I get the feeling my mom would be proud.

My dress pools onto the grass. I stride knee-deep into the water, seizing up momentarily at the chill, then relaxing as my body adjusts to the temperature. I teeter for a moment, the water lapping just beneath my kneecaps, see-sawing with that timeless debate—enter slowly, or all at once?—and then I decide: all at once.

I submerge myself completely, feeling my toes graze the bottom of the pool, then kick up and burst through the surface.

The first thing I see is Ren, framed by sunlight, peeling off his T-shirt so he can join me. He's barefoot now, running one hand through his hair to loosen the messy topknot samurai-bun. Thick, choppy locks half-cover his eyes, and I wonder, hungrily, if that's what he looks like when he first wakes up in the morning. Loose and messy. Unfairly sexy without even trying. I wouldn't mind seeing that sight like a million-billion-zillion times in a row. My imagination frolics down a sensuous path. I feel heat flushing my cheeks.

He moves towards the edge of the water and asks me, "How deep?"

I somehow manage to freeze and blush simultaneously. How ... deep?

"Um . . ." I reply, dog-paddling in place, wondering if he can read my racing thoughts.

He gestures at the water. "How deep is it? Can I dive?"

Oh. Right.

"Not very deep. Maybe four and a half feet. At least where I'm standing."

He kicks off his shoes, then his jeans, and I try, I mean *really* try, not to gawk at the impressive situation that's going on in his burgundy-colored boxer-briefs. I try. But I fail.

He strides smoothly into the water like a hot knife gliding through butter. Barely even flinches when the brisk iciness splashes his toned midsection, ribcage, and chest. He dips beneath the surface and remerges with his black hair slicked back, shaved sides exposed.

I am doddering in place, half standing, half dog-padding, doing my best not to faint from sensory overload. He glides over to me with a skilled breaststroke, catches me around my waist, and pulls me close.

The warmth of our bodies contrasts deliciously
with the coolness of the water. I kiss him lightly,
almost imperceptibly, on the collarbone. He shivers.
Growing bolder, I plant a light kiss on the side of his
neck, midway between his shoulder and earlobe. He
grasps my waist tighter in response. One more kiss,
just beneath his jawline. I am aching for his lips, feeling
greedy and frenzied, and yet I don't want to rush this
exquisite moment.

Apparently, neither does he.

"Tell me something about yourself," he asks softly.

"What do you want to know?"

"Well, let's start with … what made you decide to
create a dating profile?"

I lean into his bare chest, considering how to answer
that un-simple question. Because a purple-haired death
party planner made me do it? Because I've never tried
it before?

Because I want to give true love one last shot before
I leave this world permanently? I decide to tell him the
truth. At least, one version of it.

"I made a profile because … I want to meet my soul
mate and fall in love. True love. The kind of love that
lasts forever."

He flashes me a look of surprise.

"Too intense? Have I scared you away?" I ask him,
only half-joking.

"No," he says, and I believe him. "You just caught me by surprise. Most people aren't that … straightforward. Most people don't seem to know what they want or why they're dating. Or they know, but they're afraid to say it out loud."

"Sounds like you've had a few disappointing experiences," I press, curiously. He nods.

"You might say that," he confirms. "I've been doing the whole online dating thing for about a year. It's been … interesting," he concludes diplomatically. I can tell that "interesting" is probably code for "aggravating and possibly a waste of time."

"But what about you?" he inquires. "Dating for a long time? Newly single? Rebounding? Secretly married? What's your deal?"

"I've been single for a couple of years. I haven't dated anyone for a long time. Too long. Literally not a single person. But I've spent about one thousand hours on Netflix getting intimately acquainted with the cast of *Gilmore Girls*. If that counts for anything."

"Years?!" he thrashes the water theatrically. "I can't believe that." He raises an eyebrow suspiciously. "OK, spill it. Why have you been single for so long? Are you a serial killer? A spy? A visitor from another planet collecting data to bring home to your species?"

"Maaaybe?" I giggle. "How do you feel about anal probing?"

He blushes beet-red and it's outrageously cute.

"I might not be opposed. Under the right circumstances."

"Noted," I respond.

I submerge myself beneath the surface of the water once again, slicking my hair down my back. I can't remember the last time I swam completely naked. Maybe not since I was a kid. Naked in a semi-public place? Probably never. It's unnerving and exciting.

He paddles a few feet away, smiling broadly. The sinking sun illuminates his face in a coppery rose-gold. I swim closer, and he splashes me mischievously. I splash back. The mascara that Tasha methodically applied is probably running in rivulets down my face, but I don't care.

I've never felt this kind of instant-connection with anyone before. I honestly didn't think it was possible. This doesn't feel like a typical first date, full of bumbling awkwardness and self-conscious posturing. It's more like we're kids on the playground rushing up to each other with open hearts that have never been bruised. *"Will you play with me?" "Yes!"* Best friends forever. Simple and pure. I don't want this playdate to end.

I glide towards him and burrow myself in his arms. He smoothes down my wet hair and plants one small, unspeakably delicious kiss just above my left eyebrow.

"How long did you say you were in town for?" he asks softly.

"I didn't say," I respond, somewhat cryptically.

A beat passes, as if he's waiting for me to elaborate. I don't. Another beat.

The shrill sound of a child—giggling and glee-screaming—interrupts the silence. We hear child-sounds, grown-up banter, and footsteps crunching on the gravel path, probably less than fifty feet away. Ren instinctively moves to the side, shielding my naked body from potential public viewing.

"Um ... clothes?" he asks.

I nod.

As if to signal, *"Party's over, kids, time to move along ..."* the sun begins its descent behind the horizon. A breeze kicks up and within seconds, it feels like the temperature plummets about ten degrees. The daylight is fading, casting tree-shaped shadows across the gravel—long and inky with pointed tips like arrowheads. I shiver. Goosebumps prickle the backs of my arms.

In one sweeping motion, my entire body is plucked from the water, and I realize, dumbfounded, that Ren is carrying me towards the shore. I'm not exactly a tiny woman, but apparently he's strong enough to hoist me up in his arms with minimal effort. Not even a subtle grunt. I can feel his steely abs contracting as he moves, and I realize that this man could probably tear a phonebook in half if the spirit moved him to do so.

He releases me onto my tiptoes and whips a couple of towels out of his backpack.

Whoa. So prepared. What a Boy Scout.

Wrapping me snugly in one of the soft cloths, he towels off quickly and modestly turns away. He manages to remove his wet boxer-briefs and slip on his dry jeans without exposing himself to me. Which, I must admit, is a bit disappointing.

I follow his lead, switching into my dry sundress. We stuff our wet towels into his backpack and zip it shut, standing upright a split second before the family crunches into the clearing. The child beelines towards the water. The parents halt their conversation, taking in our sopping wet hair and flustered expressions, and give us a knowing glance.

We giggle and scurry past them, arm in arm, heading back towards the parking lot.

Ren swings the backpack straps over his shoulders and loops one arm around my waist. Leaning close, he whispers, "Your little kisses in the water were driving me insane. I want to kiss you back. Properly."

"But not here?" I respond, matching his whisper. He shakes his head.

"If you're comfortable with it, I was thinking … my place." He quickly adds, "it's not far," as if geographic distance is somehow going to influence my decision. Ha ha ha. No.

I nod emphatically, no longer bothering to try to "play it cool" or mask my enthusiasm. Kissing. Yes. Now. Please and thank you.

We practically skip back to the car. He gets the engine roaring in seconds. I rest my left hand on his right thigh as he reverses and peels out of the lot. I roll down my window to let the breeze flood over us. Even without the presence of the sun, the air feels warm, like an embrace.

"Why did you reply back to me?" I ask, smiling through damp tendrils of hair that won't stay out of my face. I'm fishing for compliments and utterly aware of it.

"On the dating site, you mean?"

"Yeah."

He turns left on 42nd Avenue and we pass the car wash, the light rail station, the liquor store. So many familiar landmarks. How is it possible, in this relentlessly neighborly city where everybody knows everybody plus everybody's brother and grandma, too, that we've never crossed paths before? Not even once?

"Well, you're absolutely beautiful," he begins. "Initially, I liked your photo. I'm sorry if that makes me shallow or whatever, but it's true."

"It doesn't," I reply. "I liked your photo, too." Uh yeah. I sure did.

"And I was seriously impressed when you messaged me with a poem. Nobody's ever done that before. Actually, women typically don't message me at all. They usually wait for me to make the first move. So, when you wrote to me like that, I was intrigued. Honestly, it made my day."

Right on Park Ave. We pass a used guitar shop, a Buddhist meditation center, a few churches, and the Midtown Greenway. Cyclists signal politely, dipping down onto the enclosed Greenway path where cars are not permitted. My mind flashes back sixteen, maybe seventeen years ago when my parents let me bike the entire length of the Greenway—without supervision—for the very first time. Five-and-a-half miles, end-to-end.

It was a crisp autumn morning, and I flew like a bird on my used Schwinn, hair whipping out from under the edges of my helmet. It was one of the first times I felt like a real "grown-up." Unattended. Liberated. Completely free. Of course, that was before the complications of actual grown-up life—job applications, bills, taxes, death, disease—cascaded into my world. That was back when choosing a hair scrunchie to match my nail polish color was the most difficult decision of my day.

I smile inwardly, lost in an imaginary conversation with my fifteen-year-old self. "Enjoy this moment," I would tell her, if I could. "Because you will never feel this exact feeling again. Your first solo-ride down the

Greenway happens exactly once. Your first kiss, your first job, all of it … your life happens exactly once. Try to keep your eyes open. Stay awake."

We're moving towards East 26th Street, and my intuition tells me he's going to hang a left at the intersection. The city landscape is embedded in my bones. Even with my eyes closed, I'd know we're moving towards the Whittier neighborhood. Ground zero for hipsters and undergrad art students paying $40,000 a year to learn graphic design and stop motion animation. Is that where he lives?

It feels liberating to not know … anything. We could be heading into Whittier, or Lowry Hill, or maybe even across the river into Saint Paul. He's behind the wheel, and there is nothing for me to do. It's strangely exciting.

"Do you want to hear another poem?" I ask.

He nods. "Absolutely. What you got for me?"

"Another one by Hafiz."

It's a short one about a leaf that floats skyward to kiss the sun and dissolves into bliss. I recite it from memory.

"Another one," he urges, giving my hand a prolonged squeeze as we pause for a red light. "One more."

I rake through my memories. I can't recall any others by Hafiz, the poet he mentioned on his dating profile, so I veer in a different direction.

I have all that I need
My work, this cup of coffee,
My world is heavy with blessings
I have no right to want,

and want and want and want . . .
And yet, small things sharpen my hunger
An embrace at the airport,
Meals perfectly portioned for two,
The story she tells breathlessly,
about the ring he chose for her to wear
He calls her, she answers,
he's on his way home
and does she need anything from the store?
"No, nothing, sweetheart, except you.
Come home. I love you."

These are the small things that agonize me
These are the small things that make me voracious and wild,
blind with longing, hasty and stupid

I have so much. I shouldn't want,
and want and want and want
This is what I tell myself in a bed that is too big
in a room that is too quiet
in a life that is heavy with blessings
I have all that I need
I repeat
I have all that I need

We stop outside a yellow brick apartment building
with a criss-cross pattern of ivy crawling up the walls.
He pulls the car into park and shuts off the ignition.

"Whoa," Ren says, tucking the keys into his
pocket. "I've never heard that one before. Who wrote
it?" he asks.

"Me."

He glances sideways at me, saying nothing,
expressionless.

My previous confidence disintegrates. Immediately,
I regret opening my mouth. It's not a good poem.
It's pretty awful, actually. Like something you'd hear
someone perform at an open mic night while you're
cringing through every line. It's too vulnerable. Nobody
wants to hear about a privileged woman's pathetic,
desperate hunger for love. This gets filed under "Things
not to do on a first date: share your sappy, neurotic
poetry with a man who previously wanted to kiss you
but probably does not anymore."

In a daze, I follow him into the apartment building,
past the yellow brick exterior, through a dark blue
door with a bronze handle. He walks down a carpeted
hallway with peculiar flowered wallpaper, up a flight
of stairs, then another, to the left, and down another
hallway. I follow.

With each step, my heart pounds anxiously in my
chest. I crossed the line. He thinks I'm desperate and

clingy. Whatever romantic fervor we experienced
earlier, I'm pretty sure it's over.

He stops in front of another dark blue door with
another bronze handle. Apartment #33.

A pair of well-worn hiking boots sit neatly outside
the doorway on a woven mat, coated with dust from
some recent adventure. I stare at them awkwardly,
pretending to be highly interested in the shoelaces.

"It's about you, right?" he asks. "The poem, I mean?"

"Yeah." Wow, those laces. So ... lacey.

I feel his hand slip behind me, cradling the small
of my back with extreme tenderness. The gesture
surprises me. Maybe I haven't completely frightened him
off just yet.

"Yeah, it's about me. I've never really been in love.
I've had relationships in the past, like pretty serious ones,
but I can't honestly say I've ever been in Love with a
capital *L*. Every relationship I've ever had, there was this
feeling like ... *you're great, like really great, but you're not
... it.* I would imagine the future, and I couldn't envision
them in it."

Ren places a soft, knee-buckling kiss on the side of
my neck. OK. He's still with me. Not bolting for the hills
yet. My confidence returns.

"I know it might be sappy and stupid, but like I said
earlier, by the waterfall, all I've ever wanted is to find my

soul mate. A real, serious, forever-and-ever kind of love. Like my parents had."

"Nora," Ren's voice is so close, I can feel the reverberations against my skin. "It's not sappy. And it's not stupid. Everybody wants love. Everybody is hungry for that kind of connection. I'm hungry for it, too."

I could be imagining it, but I think I detect the faintest hint of a growl in his tone, as if he's hungry in … a lot of different ways.

If this were a predictable Blockbuster movie, this would be the part where he pins me to door, tearing away my clothes, covering my skin with frantic kisses, before carrying me over the threshold with one arm, laying me down on a bearskin rug in front of a roaring fire. (Which was miraculously ignited by … whom? The invisible butler?)

That doesn't happen.

Instead, he quietly unlocks the door. We step inside, and he tosses his phone and keys into a ceramic dish. I take in the room. Gray couch. Black coffee table. Cheap, but nice, like IKEA probably. Yellow tea kettle. Framed poster print of *The Great Wave off Kanagawa*. Macbook Air charging on the kitchen counter. A couple of dishes in the sink. Your typical bachelor pad. Sparse, functional, with minimal ornamentation. Decently appointed, but not completely perfect, just like his car.

I can exhale here. I can relax. I like it.

He excuses himself to use the restroom. I sit down on the couch, flipping through last month's issue of *Wired* magazine. I'm halfway through an article about the future of videoconferencing when I sense his presence behind me.

I feel his hands massaging my shoulders. *Ommmmgdffgh.* After spending the night in a semi-paralyzed coma on a hospital bed, his touch feels otherworldly. He finds a crunchy knot beneath my right shoulder blade and rubs steadily. I moan.

He slips beside me on the couch, still massaging my exposed back with firm, intentional motions. He has changed into a fresh T-shirt and sweatpants that look so soft and comfortable, my skin seethes with jealousy.

The shoulder massage turns into a neck massage. The neck massage turns into hands along my jaw, in my hair, tracing the outline of my face, beckoning me to turn around. Which I do. Because I can't not.

He's sitting comfortably, cross-legged, studying me with interest.

"So, maybe we could . . ." I venture hesitantly.

And then he kisses me.

The rest of my sentence is enveloped by his mouth. I don't even know what I was planning to say anyway. But whatever it was, this is much better.

I climb into his lap, wrapping my arms around his shoulders. Our mouths, fingers, curves, and sharp

edges interlock like we were molded for one another. I
grasp at his hair. He moans into my throat, and I moan
back into his.

It's better than a romantic movie written by
Nicholas Sparks, better than any novel or TV show I've
ever seen, better than porn, yes, even that high-brow
story-driven porn that's directed by women for women.
It's the kind of kiss that makes you want to make
very bad decisions very quickly. The kind of kiss that
makes you feel like you're levitating and plummeting
simultaneously. The kind of kiss that makes you really
grateful you paid nearly $10,000 for an extra twenty-
four hours of human life. The kind of kiss that makes
God high-five his favorite angels and say, *"Now that's
what I'm talking about."*

I felt more, tasted more, experienced more, lived
more in the thirty-two seconds of my first kiss with Ren
than in the past thirty-two years of my life. It was a level
of aliveness I didn't know existed.

We migrate down a short hallway towards his
bedroom, our lips continually locked the entire time. It's
a small room with a few pairs of sneakers, a bookshelf,
a bed, and not much else. The mattress rests on a simple
wooden platform, low to the ground, Japanese-style,
with white sheets and a down comforter. The bedding
is slightly mussed because he probably wasn't expecting

company today. Encircling me in his arms, he lays me down like I am made of precious materials.

"You're so beautiful," he murmurs hypnotically, kissing me again and again.

I yank off his T-shirt and he hovers over me, straddling me, but leaving ample space between our bodies, as if he's worried about pushing too hard and too fast and frightening me away. Answering his unspoken question, I wrap my arms and legs around him, pulling his weight onto me, closing the gap between his skin and mine.

I wriggle out of my dress. His eyes devour me.

"This is my favorite part of you," he says, grabbing a handful of my ass.

"Nope, I was wrong, actually … this," he counters, kissing the crease where my hip meets my right thigh, sending me into a spasm of delicious shudders. "OK, I lied, this part is my favorite," he says, this time kissing the side of my left breast. Then the right.

"Wait, no, maybe this." He kisses the soft skin just below my belly button. "It's just too hard to decide. You're so goddamn pretty. Pretty and sweet and smart."

I let him explore me like this, melting under every kiss, drunk on his attention.

"So … you kinda like me?" I ask.

"I love you," he says.

The world goes silent in the wake of his declaration. My eyes widen. Both of us stare at each other with equally stunned expressions. Neither one of us knows what to do with this information.

"I love you," he says again, more softly, cautiously, as if one wrong move might cause me to vanish from his bed completely—blown through the window like dust, like a ghost.

"I know this might sound crazy, Nora, but I feel like I've been looking for you my whole life. I can't explain why, but I feel like we just ... match. From that very first moment in the park, I felt it. I feel like we could build a life together starting right now. We could skip all the formalities, like you said earlier, and just be together. We could be happy. It could be easy. It would just ... work."

I say nothing, intoxicated by his words, silently urging him to continue.

"I feel so drawn to you. Like I belong to you. Like you're already mine," he continues, each word clear and strong. Then—maybe because I haven't responded yet, maybe because he's realizing that this is two hundred percent crazy—his confidence seems to falter. Like feet scrabbling and slipping on black ice. "I know we barely know each other," he says quickly, as if interrupting his own thoughts, "... and I know that all of this is super fast, and I'm probably freaking you out, and ..."

I kiss him, swallowing up the panicked end of his sentence. I kiss him and kiss him and kiss him. I pull him into me, grasping the back of his neck, exulting in the sensation of his lips on mine, but also, quite honestly, buying myself a few moments of time. Because what am I supposed to say to him? I mean, really?

"I think I love you too, Ren. Oh and by the way, I hope it's not a deal breaker, but ... I'll be dead in a few hours, and you'll need to contact the hospital so they can come to collect my corpse ..."

Jesus. No. I couldn't do that to him.

That's a cruel, horrific thing for one human being to do another.

But what's the alternative?

My mind devises a cruel chart of pros and cons, weighing the possible joy, risk, and pain of every possible choice.

Should I push him away? Maybe I should. Maybe that's the ethical thing to do. I could make up some excuse for leaving abruptly (*"Oh man, I totally forgot that I've got a dentist appointment like right now ... gotta go, byeeee ..."*) and walk out the door. Vanish forever. Fade into the city, never to be found.

He'll wonder what happened, of course, but he'll invent some type of rationalization and he'll make peace with it and move on. Log back online. Swipe right. Find someone new. I'll become a brief and bizarre blip in the story of his life. Soon, he'll forget about me.

Except I don't want him to forget about me. It's disgustingly selfish, but I don't.

I want his love, and I want him to feel things intensely, and I want him to miss me when I'm gone. It's sick. But that's what I want. And I hate myself for wanting it.

Creating a dating profile with Tasha was truly the stupidest idea. God, what was I thinking? Actually, I know exactly what I was thinking. I was thinking exclusively about myself—my hunger, my loneliness, my fantasy of giving true love one last chance—but I failed to consider the fact that love involves two people's hearts, not just one.

And now Ren is mixed up in this mess that I created. He's looking at me with those glistening honey eyes and just ... waiting. He's not kissing me anymore, just looking at me, piercing right into me, and every cell in his body seems to plead for an answer.

The silence is prickling with icy electricity. The silence of a room where one person says "I love you," and there's no response—that is the coldest type of silence.

I know I have to say something.

Because when someone says they love you, you can't say nothing and stare at them blankly unless you're some kind of monster.

A beat. Then another. After thirty, maybe forty seconds of hesitant silence, I feel the words coming out, pressure building inside my belly and chest, unstoppably intense.

I tell him the truth.

"Ren, I ... I feel it, too."

His eyes shine with hope—they're the eyes of boy who has just been promised a puppy and a new Nintendo and a bicycle for Christmas, and it's absolutely precious and heartbreaking and terrible.

"I think I love you too. Even though we just met, even though it makes no sense. And ... I'm scared too."

And every word is true.

The tension in his face melts away.

We curl into interlocking C-shapes, spooning closely, his body wrapped behind mine, letting these new revelations settle into our bones.

So this is how it happens.

The cruel joke. The unthinkable twist.

I have finally found the love of my life ... on the last day of my life.

Hour Thirteen

"So now what?" Ren asks softly, his lips nuzzling my ear.

Just three words, but it's the biggest question I can imagine.

A thousand possible answers swirl in my mind.

He strokes my hair, my shoulder, the curve of my waist, tracing me like a painter with a brush, memorizing my shape.

I know I have to tell him. I just don't know how to find the right words.

No, that's a lie. I know what to say. I'm just terrified that this exquisite moment will come to a shattering, devastating halt—a piano dropped from an eighty-story skyscraper onto the concrete—if I reveal the truth about who I am and how much time I have left.

I don't want to be evicted from his arms.

I can't stand the thought of seeing his eyes flash with betrayal, like I've just cradled his heart in my hands before carelessly tossing it into a blender. Set to pulse and pulverize. *Whirrrr.*

But the weight of the unspoken words threatens to crush me. I am not going to spend my final hours of life lying to myself or to the man I'm beginning to love. He deserves to know the truth. Not just the pretty parts. All of it.

So I tell him.

The words pour out of me like steam escaping a kettle. Hot, fast, unrelenting.

"There's something important I need to tell you . . ."

I start from the beginning. The heart condition. The surgery that never really began. Complications with the anesthesia. My death. Temporary Cellular Resuscitation. Waking up semi-paralyzed in the eggshell-colored hospital room with the clock insistently ticking on the wall. Orange juice that tasted like licorice. Tossing my phone in the garbage. Finding Tasha. Her scheme to set me up on a date and now ... this. Him. Us. Here.

"So that's everything," I finish.

Silence.

His pupils are wide and black, just a faint ring of gold at the perimeter. I'm panicking inside, heart pounding like a terrorized bird in a cage. He peels himself away from my body, and I nearly cry out in pain.

It's over. I knew it. Stupid, stupid, stupid. I can't blame him. I mean, I just dropped the bombshell to end all bombshells. *Hi, nice to meet you, I'm in love with you, let's live happily ever after, JK, I'm dead!*

He pulls himself into a seat on the bed, facing away from me, hunched over as if he's about to be sick. I pull the sheets up to cover myself, feeling ashamed and monstrous.

Finally, he speaks.

His voice is remarkably calm. His eyes are glistening with tears and his face is stricken, and I can tell he is using every iota of his willpower to remain steady and controlled.

"How much time do we have?" he asks.

"I totally understand if you want me to leave . . ." I mumble rapidly, twisting the sheets in agitation. "I know this is . . ."

"Don't," he says sharply. I stop babbling.

"How much time?" he repeats.

The sky is dark. I can see a slice of moonlight through his bedroom window. I guess-timate my remaining time in this body.

"About ten hours," I say bluntly.

He nods to himself. His chest is eerily still, as if he hasn't taken a breath in several minutes.

"Ten," he repeats. "Stay here. Please don't leave."

I watch him walk out of the bedroom, too slowly, as if he's sleepwalking. He makes a right at the end of the hallway and disappears. Then I hear his scream, deep and guttural, like a mourning animal. I hear ten staggeringly loud crunching sounds, fist meeting wall, wood snapping, books falling from the shelves onto the floor. Each punch more forceful than the last. One. Two.

Three. Four. Five. Six. Seven. Another howl of agony.
Eight. Nine. Ten. And then silence. Silence, except for
the faint sound of paint and plaster shivering away
from the wall.

I am awestruck, frightened, and mortified. Shame
burns inside of me. *Selfish, selfish, selfish. I did this to him. It
would be better if we'd never met. What was I thinking?*

I pull the covers up to my face, and I'm shaking,
sobbing, just a nonsensical mess of snot and self-disgust.

I hear the sound of running water. Cupboards
opening and closing. The snipping of scissors. Footsteps
in the hall.

He returns to the bedroom with his right hand
wrapped in a black cloth. His face is streaked with tears.
He returns to his position on the bed, right by my side,
as if nothing has happened. His knuckles are bleeding,
seeping around the edges of the bandage.

I reach out to touch his back, stroking softly, trying
to comfort him. He doesn't flinch.

He seems different than before he left the bedroom.
Steady. Present. Calmer. Like he just purged his fury
through his knuckles, pounding it through the wall with
each blow.

"I'm ready now," he says quietly.

"For what?" I ask nervously, even more quietly.

"I'm ready for the next ten hours. I'm ready to give
you all of myself, every part of me, if you'll have me," he

says. "It's only ten hours. I hate that it's only ten hours.
But it's better than nothing at all."

I press my lips to his chest, nodding.

"So what's your dream, Nora? How can I," his voice
cracks, tears rimming his eyes. "How can I make this,
this … the best ten hours of your life?"

I have a few ideas.

I press myself closer, skin on skin, warmth against
warmth, wriggling up towards the place where his neck
curves into his ear. I whisper exactly what I want. I hold
nothing back. I pour it out. Everything I want to taste,
feel, and experience with Ren. Everything I want to give
to him. Everything I can offer. My words are raw and
urgent. There's no shield protecting my ego. No hiding.
No censorship. Feeling his heart accelerate as I speak,
I add . . .

". . . But I don't want to pressure you. Only if
you want to."

His mouth finds mine. His hands dig into the soft
flesh of my hips, pulling me so close that I gasp.

He absolutely wants to.

Hour Fourteen

Oh . . .

Hour Fifteen

. . . My . . .

Hour Sixteen

God.

Hour Seventeen

Delirium.

It's the only accurate description for my current state of being.

My lips are raw from his urgent, unrelenting kisses. Every square inch of skin is tingling, enlivened by his touch. My temples are pounding, blood thundering in my ears. My lungs heave like an Olympic swimmer emerging from a record-breaking two-hundred-meter sprint. I'm drunk on the sensation of skin meeting skin. High on the intensity of his gaze. Every part of me, rubbed slightly raw from the hint of stubble on his jaw. Utterly spent, devastated, wrecked, yet greedy for more.

Climax after climax has reduced me to a shuddering mess. It's sad, really, but I never knew sex could be … like *this*. I've always enjoyed a pretty decent sex life—I come, he comes, goodnight kiss, roll over, pass out, everybody's happy—but this is a different echelon of sensation.

Somewhere towards the end of the third hour of delirium, our bodies spiral downwards into a natural conclusion. We sink into a tangle of limbs, facing one another, my head resting on his chest, fingers clasped, interlocking like puzzle pieces, completely entwined like we were born for one another. I feel empty yet full, exhausted yet vividly awake.

I steal a glance at his face. His eyes are closed, and the faintest smile passes across his lips. He looks peaceful. Satisfied. I wonder if, in this post-orgasmic haze, he has temporarily forgotten the grim reality of our situation. Or if he's just fighting back those thoughts, trying to be present in this moment with me.

My mind whirls through one thousand possible moments just like this one, but different. All the possible futures that could have—and should have—been ours.

Waking up together on a humid Sunday morning, lazy eyes drifting across one another's naked bodies, knowing we have no plans today, which of course, is always the best plan.

Falling asleep together after a long, dark, frigid winter night, the heat of his body pulsating on my back, locked into a horizontal embrace, protected and complete.

Slinking out of a spontaneous summer nap, late afternoon light winking through the curtains. Me, rising just a few minutes before him, preparing a tray of iced coffee, strawberries, toast with smashed avocado on top, tiptoeing back into the bedroom, teasing him awake with playful kisses, watching a grin spread across his face as he realizes what he's about to receive . . .

A thousand permutations of the joy, the
connectedness, the love that we could have. Would have
had. If only ... I wasn't ...

A wretched, agonized sob leaves my throat,
completely outside of my control. Delirium
becoming despair.

I curl into a tight, miserable fetal position, peeling
my body away from his warmth, shuddering, convulsing
with grief. I feel like an animal, completely out of
control, grieving the life we'll never share, the moments
we'll never experience, the kisses, the birthdays, the
anniversaries, the decades of old age, walking hand
in hand together. I grieve for us, for him, for me. For
everything I'll never do, taste, experience, become ...

I've cried a lot in the past eighteen hours or so. But
this is the first time that I've really, truly grieved my own
death. I cry until there is nothing left.

He doesn't try to stop me. He lets me thrash and
sob and wring everything out. I sense him behind me,
feel him shift on the bed, coming into a seated position
on top of the sex-stained tornado of pillows and sheets.
Just watching. Witnessing. Waiting, patiently, for me to
be complete.

When I'm finished, I feel empty, hollow, but it feels
good. Like I've just unloaded a lifetime of pent-up
frustration and suffering. I feel light and unburdened.
I'm just ... here. Alive. Sort of. For the time being. We

all have our ways of coping with the brutal reality of life and whatever comes after life, I guess. He needs to punch a series of holes into the wall and apparently, I need to sob hysterically every couple of hours. So it goes.

He moves off the bed onto the floor, coming into a kneeling position, his eyes level with mine, looking so goddamn handsome, and I can't help it … I smile. The last few remaining tears seep downward, and I dry my face using the corner of one of his pillow cases.

I rest my cheek on the bed. For a few moments, a few breaths, we both hold our positions in silence. Me, curled at the edge of the bed. Him, kneeling before me, quietly, worshipfully. Finally, I say the only words that make any sense:

"Ren, I love you."

He echoes the words back to me, instantly and without hesitation, replacing his name with my own.

This is a unique type of bliss I've never experienced before—the bliss of knowing that our feelings are completely aligned.

Suddenly, I feel a twinge of anxiety and compulsively glance around the room for a clock, a watch, a phone, something. I'm not panicking, but I just want to know . . .

Ren is one step ahead of me.

"Seven hours," he says, softly. "A little over seven hours remaining."

I nod, taking it in. Seven. OK. More time than I thought, actually. This is good news. I can work with this.

I exhale fiercely and make my choice:

No more tears. No more grief. I just want to live.

I want to savor every minute with this man for as long as I can.

We don't get the luxury of seven decades together like some couples do. We don't get holidays and family vacations and favorite movies and "our song" and make-up sex after a silly fight. I'll never meet his parents. He'll never watch me grow soft, creased, and wrinkled. I'll never learn what kind of father he might be. He'll never tell me how his love for me has only grown deeper and stronger than he ever thought possible on our fortieth anniversary. We'll never get to spoil our grandkids with an unreasonable number of birthday presents. Never. We don't get the privilege of a lifetime together. But we have seven hours. And I'll be damned if we don't use every single minute to the fullest.

I lean over the edge of the bed and kiss him fiercely. He reaches up to cradle the back of my neck with one hand, grasping my hair. I feel warm again, like there's a sun inside my chest.

"Ren … I have a really important question."

He leans back on his heels.

"Yes?"

He braces himself for my question, eyes wide, no doubt worrying that I'm about to reveal some other horrific piece of news, even worse than the last time.

"I am starving. Do you have any food?"

Relief floods his face. He laughs. Clambering back onto the bed, he showers my bare shoulders with small kisses. And then slaps my ass fiercely. Guess I deserve that.

"I happen to be an incredible cook. I'm so glad I get a chance to show off for you."

"Oh yeah?" I giggle, wrapping myself around him, luxuriating in the sensation of skin on skin once again. "What's your specialty?"

"Pancakes," he replies matter-of-factly.

There is something about the seriousness of his tone—contrasted with the silliness of the word "pancakes"—that tilts me into a fit of giggles. He responds with a smile that lights up the room. It's that special kind of smile that a man gets when he knows he's done something to please his woman, and he's proud and enchanted and wants nothing more except to do it again.

"Pancakes, huh?" I say, amidst lingering hiccup-like giggles. "Show me what you got, hotshot."

He's already bounding towards the kitchen. No time to waste.

Hour Eighteen

With staggering speed, he assembles all of the essentials.

Flour. Eggs. Milk. Butter. Salt. A pint of fresh blueberries. Real maple syrup—the kind that comes from a tree, not an artificial goo factory.

I have no idea what time it is outside, but in here, in our sacred world, it feels like Sunday morning.

I sidle up to a barstool next to the kitchen island. I'm wearing one of his white T-shirts and a pair of boxers that I found in his bedroom—disgustingly cliché, I know, the "whole borrowing your boyfriend's clothes" dealio, but I desperately want his scent all over me.

He pours me a glass of grapefruit juice, and his eyes widen as I lift my shirt—his shirt—to flash my bare chest at him, for no particular reason. I do a sultry little dance in my seat, swiveling my hips on the barstool, all while sipping my juice casually like nothing unusual is happening whatsoever. I feel giddy and brazen.

"Do that again . . ." he warns playfully. "And pancakes will be postponed indefinitely." I make a taunting "oooh" sound in reply, downing the rest of my juice.

He's busying himself with various measuring cups, bowls, whisks, and whatnot, and he's not wearing a shirt—which is cruelly distracting. His sweatpants are resting low across his hipbones, exposing the full length of his hypnotically sexy torso. It's like D'Angelo in that one music video where he's singing with those, you know, hipbone-muscle-thingies all exposed, and it's just like "Whoa." Google it.

If this were a TV show on *The Food Network*, the women (and quite a few men) in the audience would be shrieking and fanning themselves in complete hysterics, and quite possibly chanting and babbling and speaking in tongues. Panties would fly onto the stage. Security would need to escort numerous audience members out of the room.

"Can I help?" I ask, ostensibly to accelerate the cooking process, but really because I just want to be close to him in the kitchen, grazing our hips together, side by side, as we work.

"Can you separate eggs?" he asks. I nod.

"Eggcellent," he responds, and we both start giggling at this ridiculous pun.

"Ren, wait, hold on a sec … are you secretly … a total dork?" I ask, gasping in mock astonishment.

"Takes one to know one."

"Touché."

He hands me a cardboard container of brown Grade-A's. "Yolks here, whites in this one. Four total."

We zest lemons, rinse berries, beat eggs into a furious, foamy lather, butter the griddle and attend to all of the other necessary preparations, pausing only to lay spontaneous trails of kisses on each other's jawlines and cheeks. And other places.

Ren eyes the bowl of batter and determines that it's a bit too dry and needs at least one more egg. He instructs me to separate a few more. I accidentally drop a shrapnel of eggshell into the batter and receive a swift, stinging spanking—boxers pulled down, hand meeting bare skin, bent flat with my chest pressed onto the prep table—in return. It happens so fast, I don't even have time to yelp. I glance back over my shoulder and see Ren's eyes blazing hungrily.

"Watch those shells. Don't get careless," he warns me, in a mock-threatening tone. I can tell he's just playing, and yet, his deep voice awakens something inside of me—like a treasure chest unlocking. *Click.* I want to play, too.

Impulsively, I grope forward and grab a fresh egg from the container. He watches as I raise my hand, and then—in an act of wild rebellion—smash it down on the counter, mere inches from the bowl of blueberry-studded pancake batter. Yolk oozes grotesquely through my fingers. Shell fragments litter the counter. So wrong. Chaos. Disaster.

He mock-gasps in horror and consternation. I stifle a giggle.

He slaps my ass again, harder this time, then yanks me backwards and flips me to face him. Pinning my arms above my head, he backs towards the wall until my shoulder blades connect with the wood. Then he's kissing me, firmly, intensely—neck, collar bone, lips—tasting traces of grapefruit juice and dried tears.

He whispers to me in a theatrically menacing voice:

"So, so careless. Will I have to punish you to teach you a lesson?"

OK. Hello. This pancake-making process just took a seriously *Fifty Shades* twist.

His voice pins me into place. My cheeks flush and my neurons fire wildly, unsure if his little performance is seriously sexy, or seriously silly, or both. But I definitely don't want him to stop.

"Maybe, um, yes? Maybe I need ... lessons?" I squeak in response, half-stifling another giggle.

I get the distinct feeling that even if we had seven hundred years together, Ren would never stop surprising me. Never stop revealing intoxicating new depths, new desires, unexpected facets of his personality ...

He moves closer, eyes full of promises, just as an angry, metallic shriek brings our reverie to an abrupt ending. Ren backs away quickly, fanning the air, flipping knobs on the stove. The smoke detector rages and I cover my ears until he finds the switch and flicks it off.

A charred pan of bacon sits on the stove—black, sooty, completely inedible. We'd forgotten all about it.

He slides the pitiful pan into the sink, turning on the cool tap to extinguish the charred mess. Moving towards the edge of the kitchen, further away from the smoke, our hands intertwine and we kiss. I can feel a shift. The performance has ended. No more tough guy, no mock threats of punishment, no Christian Grey persona. Now it's just Ren.

His hands roam to the small of my back, my waist, then up to cradle my face.

"I want forever with you," he half-sobs, half-moans, kissing me again. I can't tell if he's angry, resentful, mournful, or overwhelmed with lust. Maybe all of the above.

If I could put this exact moment—surrender, sweetness, the bitter scent of overcooked bacon, his sweat, his kisses, the faint salt taste of our tears, his murmured *"I love you"*—on instant-reply for all eternity, I would.

Maybe, in a few hours, once I cross over into whatever comes next, I will be able to do that. Maybe death is just an unlimited playlist of all your favorite moments from life. The greatest hits. Over and over. As long as you want. The thought feels comforting to me. But I don't have time to wonder about that, and frankly, it seems pointless to do so, because nobody really knows what comes next. At least, I don't. I don't have a clue.

All I have is what's right here in front of me: a beautiful man, a bowl of batter that desperately needs griddling, and hopefully some more bacon that we can fry up. Properly, this time.

Hour Nineteen

I am suddenly, and somewhat pungently, aware that I haven't showered in several days. It's not particularly cute. As much as I love watching Ren flip pancakes with authoritative grace, I excuse myself and head into his bathroom for a quick rinse-off.

His shower is outfitted with unscented soap, shaving cream, a nice-looking razor, and not much else. Everything you need. Nothing you don't.

As the hot water pounds onto the nape of my neck, I wonder, momentarily, what "our" place might look like if we converged our lives together. After a few seconds of interior design fantasies, I curtail that train of thought because … there's no point.

Toweling off, I will myself to think about something else. Is this why all those monks are constantly practicing meditation? So their minds don't drift into painful and irrelevant places every five seconds? If so, I could really use that superpower right now.

I change into an oversized T-shirt that says Midwestern Karate Association and plop back onto the barstool, watching as Ren makes the final flourishes to our very belated breakfast.

He drizzles a short stack of ludicrously photo-worthy pancakes with warm maple syrup, sprinkles a few extra berries on top, and adds a light dusting of powdered sugar. The grand finale: a pat of creamy butter on top. It's practically pornographic.

OK. Make that *absolutely* pornographic. The first bite of maple-and-butter-drenched pancakes rips me into a new stratosphere of pleasure. Each forkful is studded with warm blueberry jewels, perfectly proportioned, bursting into my mouth.

"You were not kidding," I sigh, sidling closer to him on my stool, so that our knees touch. "You are an incredible cook."

"Do you believe in reincarnation?" he responds as I'm enjoying an exceptionally exquisite bite of pancake with a chunk of crisp bacon on top. I'm taken aback by his question.

"If I say 'yes,' does that mean I get to be reborn as … a professional pancake tester?" I joke, waving a forkful around in the air. "Because that would be a pretty fantastic life."

"Seriously though," he says. "Do you?"

"Um, well … not really," I say. "I don't believe in reincarnation. I mean, I believe that when you die, your body decomposes and you re-join the earth, feeding flowers and trees or whatever, but I don't believe that you get 'reborn' as another person," I clarify.

"That's it?" he counters. "That's all we become? Plant food?"

"Well, we don't have any reason to believe otherwise, right? I mean, where's the proof that there's something 'beyond' this current existence?"

He gazes at me thoughtfully, as if that's not such a simple question. I continue, feeling my pulse rise.

"I'd love to believe that there's something more, something beyond this life—trust me, I've often wished that I had faith in something like that—but I think we tell ourselves fairy tales about heaven, reincarnation, and things like that, because we're too afraid to face the brutal truth that when it's over, that's it. It's just over."

"Nobody wants the party to end," I continue as he listens, silent and stoic. "But eventually, it does. It's easier to lie to ourselves, easier to convince ourselves that the fairy tales are true, rather than just deal with the total, crushing over-ness of it all. You live. You die. Plant food. The end."

He listens as I reach my definitive finale, patiently nodding.

"What about you? Do you believe in reincarnation?" I say, after a long-ish pause.

"Would it surprise you if I said that … I don't?" he returned, slicing his final pancake in half and placing one half on my plate, practically floating atop a pool of molten maple syrup.

I eye him curiously.

"I don't believe in reincarnation, not in the literal, die-and-come-back-as-a-new-baby sense," he continues, watching with a smile as I slice my final pancake into four sections, compiling four miniature bacon-pancake towers. "But I do believe that there is 'something' waiting after this lifetime. And I believe that eventually, with the right scientific advancements, we will discover what is waiting."

I listen as he continues, raising one last forkful to my mouth.

"Gravity. The wheel. Skyscrapers. Penicillin. Space flight. Postponing death. Prolonging life. Understanding what comes after this life. Everything is incomprehensible and impossible ... until one day, it's not."

He stands to clear away the dishes, stacking them in the sink and giving the countertop a brisk sweep with a damp cloth.

He continues, "The fact that you are here with me—that is a miracle of science that would not have been possible even ten years ago. Not long ago, we didn't even know that a procedure like Temporary Cellular Resuscitation was possible. But here we are. Eating pancakes. Living inside of a miracle."

I nod. He has a point.

"Maybe someday, you and I will reunite inside another type of miracle."

He eyes intensify, locking with mine.

He seems to be waiting for me to respond, to agree, disagree, do anything other than just stare at him blankly.

After a few beats of silence, I rise off the barstool, move closer, and kiss him. His arms instinctively encircle me. I can't enthusiastically voice my agreement, but I don't have to dash his hopes either.

The best I can offer him is a wobbly, uncertain kind of optimism.

"I really hope that what you believe—that you and I will be reunited, somehow, somewhere—I hope that turns out to be true."

He pulls me closer into his body, burrowing his face in the curve of my neck. We rock subtly, swaying, barefoot in the kitchen. Saying nothing. Feeling everything.

The second hand of the clock mounted on the wall ticks softly—an aggravating, insistent reminder.

I tilt my chin upwards and find Ren gazing down at me. Lips curled in a smile. Eyes warm, molten with affection. He runs his fingers up the sides of my waist and ribcage, sending me into a subtle flurry of shivers. His kiss lands on me, sending the world into slow motion.

He seems to be inhaling me with each unbroken kiss, folding into the next kiss, trying to absorb my scent, my taste, my being into himself. I feel a drunken head rush as he lifts me into his arms, my legs wrapping around his waist as he carries me back towards the bedroom. I can feel his heart beating steadily through the thin fabric of his T-shirt. Can feel my own heart beating in time.

A pressure builds inside my chest, like I'm sinking fast, underwater, holding my breath . . .

And then ... it's all wrong.

I feel a sickly heat overwhelm my body. Heaviness. Pressure in my lungs. A boulder on my heart. I rip my face away from Ren's next kiss, feeling like I'm about to release my pancakes onto the floor behind him.

The pressure in my chest builds and builds, like a grand piano is resting on top of me. I try to gulp down some air, but it doesn't help. Instinctively, I twist my torso, shake out my arms, as if I can shudder this heavy, ominous feeling right out of my body.

My arms begin to tingle. The tingling spreads to my back, neck and jaw. I feel myself going dizzy, going black, going gray, going down as my knees buckle beneath me . . .

No.

Not yet.

I'm not ready yet . . .

Hour Twenty

"Nora, Nora, are you with me? Nora, talk to me. What are you feeling?" Ren's voice sounds disembodied and distant, even though his lips are just inches from my face.

He's gotten me onto the bed, propped semi-upright, pillows arranged behind my neck for support. He's cradling my face in his hands. He seems tightly wound, coiled, ready to spring into action, and I can see fear glittering in his wide-open eyes.

I feel unbelievably exhausted, as if every single cell of my body has collapsed inward. I gesture limply at my chest.

"Hurts. Heavy," I manage to choke out.

Ren departs briefly, returning with cool, damp towels from the bathroom. He lays one over my forehead, another behind my neck. I sigh. I hadn't realized that I was sweating. The coolness feels good. I relax. The pressure on my chest seems to dissipate slightly.

Still bad but not unbearable.

"Nora, I think you might've had a heart attack," Ren says, arranging another damp cloth across my chest. I suspect he's trying to stay exceptionally even-keeled for my benefit.

"Or some other heart issue? A stroke? I don't know. I'm going to call 9-1-1."

"No," I splutter. He freezes, phone already poised in his hand.

"No," I repeat, a little more steadily. He gives me an indecisive glance, as if he's trying to decide whether or not I'm capable of making this kind of decision right now.

"Look. My heart is messed up. I already know that. But I don't want to go to the hospital," I plead. "They'll just hook me up to machines, run tests, everything . . ." I wriggle myself so that I'm sitting fully upright on the bed, as if to show him, *Look at how healthy I am! Ta-da! No doctors required.*

"Ren, I don't want ... I just don't want to spend my final hours in a hospital with strangers. I want to be here. With you."

His face looks tortured, caught in an impossible decision with no desirable outcome no matter which choice he makes. I know exactly what he's thinking. He doesn't even have to speak. *But what if you die right here, right now ... ? And there's nothing I can do?*

He eyes me solemnly, saying nothing, still holding his phone in one hand. Three taps on the keypad and an ambulance will come surging to his street, strangers will flood into the apartment, and they'll carry me

away, taking me away from him forever. No. I can't let
that happen.

"It's probably nothing to worry about," I tell him.
"It's normal TCR stuff." And actually, that might be
true. The physicians warned me about unpredictable
reactions that might arise during the final hours of my
TCR experience. Lethargy. Dizziness. Fever. Tightness
in the chest. Maybe a fun little epileptic seizure for good
measure. All "normal" sensations as your body begins to
shut down ... for the second and final time.

Some people get these "exit symptoms," as they're
euphemistically labeled. Others don't. Some only get
them during the final hour. Others, sooner. I guess I'm
one of the unlucky ones.

Ren puts down his phone, which sends a rush
of relief across my body. He won't call. They won't
cart me away.

"How can I make you more comfortable? What can I
do?" he asks. His eyes are fiery and pleading.

"Can we just ... get out of here?" I reply softly. I feel
a sudden, intense urge to get out of the apartment, out
into the fresh air, as if a change of scenery will delay
the inevitable.

"Can we go somewhere?"

He looks like he is about to shake his head, but he
stops himself. "Where do you want to go?" he asks.

I think it over. It's nighttime—right smack in the middle of the night, actually—and the city is dark and inactive. Our options are limited to: a twenty-four-hour diner, a public park that's probably filled with unsavory characters getting up to hijinks that I don't particularly want to witness, a strip club, or, I don't know, trespassing into someone's backyard to sneak into their pool? None of these possibilities sound appealing. And then ... I know. I know exactly where I want to go.

"Ren ... where do you work? Can you take me to your job? I want to see where you spend your days. I want to see your regular, normal life."

He laughs.

"I teach martial arts for a living. You want to go to the dojo? Like right now?"

I nod as emphatically as a woman who has recently suffered a minor heart attack-ish type of thing can nod.

He presses a kiss onto my forehead, still damp from the towel he just removed, and tells me exactly what I'm hoping to hear.

"We can do that. Wait right here."

He scoots off and returns with a pair of white pants—the bottom half of a Gi uniform, I'm guessing—which feel like hospital scrubs but so much softer. I'm still sluggish and slightly unsteady, with jelly legs and a troubling heart rhythm that feels too slow at times, too fast at others, and flat-out spastic in between. He helps me out of bed, and I shoo him off, wanting to prove that I'm totally capable of putting karate pants on by myself, thank you very much.

I adjust the drawstring waist around my hips. They feel lived in, worked in, like he's worn them about four hundred times before. I like feeling pieces of him so close to me. He hands me another loose T-shirt. This one is light gray with blocky, black lettering.

Voltage Coffee.

I smile. Voltage is one of my favorite local spots to grab a scone and work on my laptop. I wonder how many times I've gone there over the past ten years. How many times he has visited, too—and if our paths have ever crossed before. Maybe so. Maybe not. Maybe I'd been focused on my screen, never glancing up to notice him. Maybe he'd been in a hurry, rushing to teach a class or get to an appointment and hadn't seen me. Maybe we'd been just twenty feet away from one another, dozens of times, submerged in our own private worlds, never seeing each other. Him, at the counter, ordering an iced tea on a hot summer afternoon. Me, bent over my computer, or lost in a book, idly sipping a coffee, contemplating my third refill. My mind flows into alternate storylines, other lives we might have lived, if we'd met sooner, in a different time . . .

"Ready?" he asks, hovering in the doorway, interrupting my reverie. "So ready."

We make our way out of the building, walking at an octogenarian speed. He loops one arm around my waist, pulling me close, supporting me as we step a few paces, rest, then a few more, another pause.

"It's not far, just a couple of blocks," he explains. "Think you can make it?"

I nod. The cool night air feels invigorating. My lungs respond, filling more deeply than before. It's that elusive, perfect temperature where you don't need to wear a sweater, yet just brisk enough to prickle your skin and awaken your body. I feel my heartbeat re-settling into normalcy, my strength returning, and I pick up the pace.

"You look really cute in that T-shirt," he tells me. I liquefy with pride, because even if I was bleeding out from a gunshot wound, lying on the concrete, if he told me I looked cute doing it, I'd be stoked.

Girl-brains are weird.

We pass stately Victorian houses and a couple of vintage-looking apartment buildings, similar to Ren's. Some with red brick. Some yellow. Ivy crawling up the sides. Art Deco insignias and bronze lettering marking the addresses.

We turn a corner and emerge onto a deserted commercial street. There's a laundromat—closed, of course. A public library. Also closed. A bus stop with one lone, solitary woman in a white button-down shirt and black slacks slumped, waiting wearily with heavy shoulders. Probably just getting off her night shift, aching to get home and rest. She gives us a wan smile with a half-nod as we pass. We smile back.

I smell the unmistakable scent of warm cinnamon rolls as we pass a bakery. Closed.

Darkened. But bustling with activity in the back kitchen. I can imagine the night-shift bakers hard at work, blinking sleepily, blasting music to stay alert, preparing for the busy morning rush in just a few hours' time.

So many people. So many lives. Sleeping. Walking. Waiting for buses. Baking rolls. Jostled together in this strange urban grid. All just trying to do ... what, exactly? Stay alive? Live another day? Eat another cinnamon roll? Find love, maybe? And keep it?

Before my mind trails too far away, Ren gives my waist a firm squeeze, gesturing towards a double-sided glass door with Japanese lettering.

"We're here," he announces, tapping a security code into a keypad to bring us inside.

It's one large room. Blonde wood floors. White walls. In the back corner, there's a registration desk with a slew of trophies behind it, gleaming faux-gold, arranged neatly and framed in a glass case. I walk in slowly, kicking off my shoes instinctively because I'm pretty sure that's what you're supposed to do in a dojo. Ren does the same.

Detaching from his side, I move into the darkened dojo, as if in a dream. I scan the walls and notice a series of framed posters and photographs. Ren bowing to an elderly sensei with soft gray hair. Ren soaring through the air, one leg extended, one leg bent, like an action movie superstar. Ren teaching kids how to karate-chop a wooden block into two chunks—I remember seeing that photo in his online dating profile, hours ago. God. Was it only a few hours ago that we first met? It feels like another universe, another lifetime.

Then there's a group photo. Ren framed by dozens of students—all different ages, different skill levels, presumably, judging by the multi-colored belts that they wear. A few other instructors stand on either side of him. A stout, older man, nearly bald, with a broad grin. A slim, red-headed woman with a high ponytail. All wearing the traditional white *Gis*. Am I just imagining it, or is the red-headed woman gazing longingly in Ren's direction instead of looking directly into the camera?

I feel a twinge of jealousy, followed by a wave of *are-you-serious-right-now* stupidity. I have no right to feel jealous of a woman that I don't know, that I will never meet, who may or may not have a crush on a man I've know for a scant handful of hours. It's ridiculous. And yet, I can't help feeling what I feel. Jealousy is a funny beast. Irrational and primal, unwilling to listen to reason.

I continue scanning the walls, trailing my fingers along each photo, each frame, wanting to memorize this room—this one-room world that my lover inhabits for the majority of his waking hours. I just want to know it.

I arrive at the final photo in the sequence. It's a sweet photo of Ren smiling broadly with a small plaque below it, which reads: Founder and Studio Director. He looks a bit younger in the photo, though not by much. I'd guess it was taken a few years earlier at most. I feel a flutter of pride. He's a business owner, a studio director, and apparently a wooden block-chopping master, all at such a relatively young age. And judging by the photos, he's adored by his colleagues and students. Seriously impressive.

These photos—tantalizing glimpses into his world— spark a greedy fire in me. I want more details, more stories, more information. I want to know everything about him.

"So, AikidoGuy82," I begin, settling myself into the chair behind the registration desk as if I own the place. "Tell me how you got into martial arts. Start from the beginning."

Ren flicks on a few light switches to illuminate the room a bit more. Not too bright, just pleasantly dim, like candlelight.

He perches on the edge of the desk, leaning back to press his palms down behind him, making his chest look even broader than usual. It's a good look.

"Not too much to tell," he responds, his gaze drifting across the half-lit room, then back at me. "As a little kid, I got obsessed with Bruce Lee movies. I'd watch them over and over until I could recite every line of dialogue by heart. I got into the habit of kicking my mom's chairs, jumping off the couch, trying to do backflips off the kitchen table . . ." he chuckles. I giggle, too. I can totally envision a miniature-sized Ren terrorizing his mother with wild lunges and leaps through their home.

"Eventually, my mom enrolled me in a kiddie program at a local dojo. I think she was grateful to have somewhere to drop me off after school, somewhere where I could expel some of my energy without destroying the furniture," he continues.

"I studied karate, first, and then aikido. I kept with it. Marched along. Earned a couple of black belts," he adds, as if it's no big deal. "Martial arts gave me structure— somewhere to direct all of my energy. It taught me discipline, respect, honor, balance . . ." he adds, "You know. All the stereotypical clichés that you might expect. I just love it. It's that simple. So now, I teach others."

"And you own this studio? You run the place?"

He nods, standing and moving towards a wooden crate filled with pillows, bolsters and mats. He pulls everything out, arranging them artfully on the wooden floor, creating an impromptu pillow-nest. He plops down, pats the empty space beside him, and gestures for me to join him.

"It's not much. Just a single room. Me plus two other instructors. But our classes usually fill up and our students tend to remain for many years. Running a small business is tough, but we do well enough," he says humbly. He's sitting cross-legged, so I mirror him, arranging myself so that our knees touch.

"I think at least one part of our bodies should be touching at all times," I say, shifting the conversation entirely.

He grins.

"I agree."

He clasps my hands in his, kissing my knuckles.

"Anyway. Enough about me. I want to talk about you. Who are you? I love you, that much I know. But I barely know you. Which is crazy."

"Not crazy," I respond, because the feeling is entirely mutual. When two people are crazy together in the same way, it cancels out the crazy. "Just ... major-league wonderful."

His face warms as I reference the poem that initially drew us together.

"I know that you love poetry, and pancakes, and skinny-dipping underneath waterfalls . . ." he teases. "So, what else? Tell me something. Tell me everything."

I sigh audibly. Everything? For the second time in less than twenty-four hours, I find myself being forced to sum up my entire life, my entire thirty-two years of existence, in a handful of sentences. First in Tasha's office—providing fodder for the dating profile she crafted for me. And now this.

Where to begin?

I decide to keep it simple.

"I like to draw. More like doodle, really. I never made art professionally, but I often thought about it. I like to write, too. But I never did that professionally either. I kinda hopped from job to job. Mostly waitressing, which I'm actually pretty good at. And hostessing. Being a barista. Serving coffee. Things like that. Hmm. What else . . ."

My voice trails off. Compared to him, I feel like an unfocused dabbler who never realized her potential. *"Nora is so bright, if only she would apply herself . . ."* comes the echoing voice of every schoolteacher I ever had, booming in my mind. And despite Tasha's very generous assessment of me—as a "daymaker"—privately, I still believe that all of those teachers were probably right. I didn't focus. I didn't apply myself. Not to anything. Not really. Unlike Ren, I am not, and never will be, a black belt in anything.

I'm sinking into an oily puddle of self-criticism, but Ren seems unaware. He's nodding as if everything I'm saying is delightful and fascinating and eagerly prods me to continue.

"Tell me about your friends."

"My friends? Well, most of my closest friends don't live here—they all went off to college in other states, got married, had kids, and all that. Our lives separated. I don't have very many close friends left here in town. None, actually. Aside from random people I've worked with, here and there . . ."

I didn't think it was possible, but yup ... this summary of my life just became even more depressing.

I'm grateful when he prompts me with a new question. "Tell me about ... what you love."

My back is pressed into his chest. He cradles me with one arm, using the other to stroke my hair tenderly. I lean into his warmth and comforting solidity, completely soothed by his embrace. As his heart beats steadily into my spine, I feel protected from the world, like nothing could ever hurt us.

"I love my mom. I love my dad, even though he's gone. I love coffee. I love poetry. I love drawing. I love beautiful things. Pretty paper, candles, girly stuff like that. I love getting lost inside of a story, whether it's a

TV show or a book or just a random person telling me their life story at the airport for no particular reason. I love making people smile. I love surprising people with gifts. I love giving compliments. I love throwing surprise parties. I love *people*, period. If there's one thing I'm really good at it, I guess it's making someone's day a little better, a little brighter than it was before. At least, that's what I try to do."

He gives me a squeeze. "You certainly made mine."

I blush. He can probably see the pink creeping all the way around to the back of my neck.

"Next question: what is your worst quality, and what is your best quality?"

I smile. I typically don't enjoy talking endlessly about myself, but I'm enjoying Ren's playful interrogation. I can tell he's listening to every word that I say so attentively, almost sensuously, as if he wants to lap up every drop.

"Worst quality: I'm easily distracted. Best quality: I'm very punctual."

"Punctuality? That's your best quality?" he teases, nudging my ribs and driving me to the edge of a tickle meltdown.

"Yes! Haaa. Nooo, stop." I swat his arms away.

"Well, I happen to find punctuality very, very sexy," he informs me, nibbling the space just behind my ear. "But you forgot about the part where you're beautiful, loving, open-hearted, playful, sexy, and so incredibly courageous."

I stiffen at his compliments. It just sounds like … too much.

"Courageous … ?" I trail off. That's not an adjective I would typically choose to describe myself.

"Yes," he confirms, his voice soft but insistent. "You chose to rise from death to live again, without knowing how it would feel or what might unfold. That is a very brave thing to do. You chose to go on a date with me, spontaneously, just to pursue the possibility of connection one last time. You chose to open yourself up to adventure, even with limited time and no guarantees that anything would pan out the way you had hoped. You allowed yourself to love me, immediately and fiercely, with no reservations. You shared your fears and greatest hopes with me."

He pulls me close, wrapping his arms completely around me.

"Do you know how many people go their entire lives without ever doing even one of those things? Do you know how many people live and die with their hearts closed tight like a fist? In just a few hours, you have shown more courage than many people display in an entire lifetime."

I've never thought of myself as particularly courageous. I always thought I was an underachiever—

smart but disappointing, creative but directionless. But hearing his words, I feel a flicker of understanding. Maybe I haven't seen myself clearly. Maybe, in my own way, I'm stronger than I thought.

"You make me feel like … I am … a special person." I say, falling into his chest. I can barely believe the words coming out of my mouth. I feel sheepish. Stupid, even.

"You are," he says, covering me with kisses. "I hope you know that. I hope you never forget."

It's funny how it takes something so dramatic— cancer, a car crash, a near-death experience, or actually dying—before things become simple, vivid, and clear. Before we can appreciate what really matters—the small moments of pleasure, the taste of maple syrup and butter, the smoothness of a beautifully swept floor, the warmth of someone's embrace—and the truth of who we really are. I didn't see it. My eyes were half-fogged. Now I'm awake. And I just wish it had happened sooner.

Hour Twenty-One

He doesn't say it, and I don't say it either. But we're both thinking the same thing.

Three hours left.

What should we do with this time?

As much as I like the idea of Ren bending me over his gleaming, perfectly polished desk and ravaging me all over again, I don't think my body could take that right this second. I am thoroughly spent.

I find myself strolling over his desk, nonetheless, as if tugged by invisible cords. An idea strikes me.

"Ren, do you have any paper?" "Of course."

He comes to my side and rummages through one of the desk drawers, removing a stack of crisp, ivory paper and a few pens.

I gather up the supplies and retreat to the pillow-nest he'd created earlier. He follows.

"I have a few people I'd like to write to," I explain. "If I give you their addresses, will you make sure these get delivered?"

He nods.

"I'll make sure. I would be honored."

I roll onto my stomach, propped onto my elbows with a fan of papers in front of me. I uncap one of the pens and formulate my thoughts. Ren arranges himself on the floor, lifts one of my feet into his hands, and begins to rub the center of my arch with decadent pressure. Slow, intentional circles swiveling upwards into the spaces between my toes.

After giving each foot a generous amount of attention, he works his way up my calves, to my inner thighs, and all I can think to myself is *"Mmmmfffnggh"* because his touch strips my vocabulary right out of my brain.

Eventually, he settles onto his side, propped up on one elbow, studying me in the semi-dim light. I reach for a pen and tap the tip against my temple a few times. An old habit that formed I don't even know when. Automatic pilot. Tap tap tap with the tip against my bare skin. As if summoned by a knock at the door, my thoughts return.

There's moonlight, white walls, bare floors, a sheaf of paper, the pressure of Ren's form against mine, and in the sparseness of this space, I find all of the words that I need to say.

Mom,

You might not remember, but recently, I called you on the phone and I asked,

"If you only had a few hours to live, what would you do with that time?"

You told me:

"Chocolate cake, champagne, and multiple orgasms. Possibly all at once if time is running short."

Well, I want you to know that I listened to your advice. It wound up being blueberry pancakes instead of chocolate cake and juice instead of champagne, but the multiple orgasms part I definitely handled, spot on.

I know this might be oversharing, but we've always had that type of relationship—no boundaries and slightly inappropriate topics. It's one of the things I love most about you.

I know we've had our disagreements though the years. I know I've disappointed you at times, and I've made you proud at others. I know I should have visited you more often in California, and I'm sorry I didn't. I hope you can forgive me.

What I really want to say is that I love you. You shaped me into the woman that I am. From you, I got my compassion, my curiosity about people's lives and feelings, my lifelong appreciation of mascara, and my willingness to try new, brave, and odd things. "You only live once!" as you always used to tell me.

Recently, someone told me that I am very courageous, and at first I didn't believe him, but then I realized that it's true—because I learned how to be courageous from you.

Also, yes, I know you didn't miss that small detail, and I know you're bursting with questions already. I didn't quite believe him. Him as in: a guy. Or, I should say, a man.

He's very tall and very strong—both physically and emotionally—and he runs his own business, which I know would impress you very much. You would really like him. He is, as you'd say, "a real hot dish."

It's possible that you'll meet him when you receive this letter. If that happens, please give him a hug from me, and if possible, ask him to make some pancakes for you and the nurses and everybody else there. You won't regret it.

I love you, mom. I won't be able to see you again, at least not in this world, but I hope—I really, really, really hope—that we'll be together again somewhere else soon.

Let's hold onto that hope.

Wherever we're going, I'll meet you there.

Your daughter,

Nora

I fold my letter into thirds and write the address of my mom's residential care facility on the top fold. I know it's not a "perfect" letter, but it's heartfelt and true. It will have to do.

I nudge the folded paper in Ren's direction.

"For my mom," I explain, pointing to the address. He nods. At this point, there's almost nothing we need to say aloud to one another. Three words and everything is understood.

I select a fresh sheet of paper and begin my second letter, smirking to myself as I write.

Tasha,

When I walked into your office—God, was it only yesterday?—I honestly had no idea what to expect.

I was frightened and disoriented. Totally desperate. You pulled me into a safe cocoon—like a magical glittery womb— and you changed everything.

Because of you, I got to meet AikidoGuy82 (his real name is Renzo, BTW) and get this … WE TOTALLY HAD SEX EVERYWHERE!!! Like … everywhere. Not just sex but a serious connection. I know it sounds crazy, but I am convinced he's my soul mate, and I met him because of you. You, and your devious, wily ways. From the bottom of my heart, thank you.

Obviously, I wish I could have met Ren sooner. I wish we had more time together. I wish a whole galaxy of things. But it is what it is. We met. We're in love. He's literally draped over me right now, and he's a million times hotter than the photo you showed me.

You were the catalyst for all of this, and I'll never be able to say "thank you" enough.

I promised I'd write a review for your new business so that you can put it on your website or Yelp or whatever. Here it is:

"I chose to purchase Temporary Cellular Resuscitation because I wanted an extra day of life. I didn't know why, exactly, I just knew that I wanted that time.

Then when my extra day arrived, I was clueless. I spent thirty minutes on Facebook, ate a cheeseburger, and felt completely aimless. I didn't know what to do with my extra time, and I could feel it slipping away like sand through an hourglass. It was the worst feeling on earth. By sheer luck, I discovered Tasha's info and hired her on the spot.

With professionalism and warmth, Tasha helped me to create the most incredible 'bonus round' day for myself. Honestly, it was the best day of my entire life.

If you're dead, if you're dying, even if you're perfectly healthy and completely alive, you need to meet Tasha Lockwood because she will propel you into doing the things you've been postponing for too long. This is a woman who understands what it means to be ... alive."

Tasha: there's your review! I hope your new business is a huge success—and I'm honored to have been your first client. Please pour yourself a glass of whatever that blue-ish booze is that you've got tucked away in your office and toast to yourself.

You're amazing.

Nora

I fold this second letter into an origami heart, because I've got a feeling Tasha will love that. I can imagine her affixing the heart to her fridge with a hot pink magnet. I don't remember her exact address, but I write her name and the general vicinity of her office on one of the heart folds. I trust that Ren is sharp enough to figure it out. He doesn't strike me as the type of guy who lacks the ability to Google shit.

I fan out several more blank pages in front of me. There are about a hundred other people that I "should" write to. My first college professor. My coworkers at my last job. The nursing team that currently takes care of my mom. Friends from high school, scattered across the country with spouses and kids.

My mind floods with names, names, names—a mental compendium of every human being who has influenced my life. I blow air through my cheeks, sighing audibly. My shoulders crunch towards my ears.

"What's up?" Ren probes, stroking my back with his free hand.

"Just trying to decide who I should write to next," I explain. "There are so many people I know I should reach out to. So many people I need to thank. So many people I should say goodbye to . . ." I'm performing mental gymnastics, tallying up all the names, pages, words, minutes. Overwhelm weighs heavily in my bones. This could take hours.

"So don't."

"Don't what?" I ask Ren, curling onto my side.

"Don't write to all of them. Or any of them. I can see that it's stressing you out, just thinking about it. So don't."

That hadn't occurred to me. Just … don't. Doing nothing is a totally valid option.

My fingers curl around Ren's waist, and relief percolates through my veins. Nothing. Nobody. That feels like the perfect choice.

"How come you make everything feel so simple?" I ask, pulling myself closer to his warmth.

"Because everything is."

Hour Twenty-Two

No. No no no.

My eyes snap wide open. Adrenaline crashes through every cell.

I feel that oddly recognizable feeling of disorientation and dread—like when you wake up in an unfamiliar hotel room, and your body can't register where you are, what day it is, and if it's morning or night. Mental pandemonium. Synapses firing incoherently. *Is it Friday or Saturday? Am I late for work? Did I miss my flight?*

Reality settles into focus.

White walls. Wood floors. Moonlight. Ren.

Ren. He's right by my side. A pair of dark honey-colored eyes meet mine.

"Did I fall asleep?" I ask, already knowing the answer. A different type of dread consumes me. I can't afford to sleep. I don't have time.

"How long?"

"About thirty minutes," he answers. "You looked so peaceful."

Part of me wants to slap him for letting me fall asleep. Now? Seriously? Unbelievable. But then he pulls me closely into his body, curling himself around me in the classic spoon-position, and all is forgiven. He rocks me gently, and despite the bare floor beneath our bodies, I feel like I could easily drift off to sleep again. Too easily.

Nearly twenty-four hours of nonstop activity is taking its toll. My eyes are heavy-lidded. I'm fighting the alluring undertow of sleep with every breath.

There's a distinct silence—the particular silence of a man gathering his thoughts, carefully selecting his words—and then Ren speaks.

"Where do you want to be … when it happens?"

It's the first time that Ren has verbally acknowledged what we both know is coming, imminently.

His voice is strained. Each word drops like a copper coin into an empty basin. "With you."

"OK. But where, though?"

"Your bed sounds like a good idea."

"Anything you want to do before then?"

"Bungee jumping?" I offer bleakly. He knows I'm kidding and gives me a firm squeeze, silently saying, *"But seriously … "*

"I really can't think of anything. Unless you want to make me the world's great cup of coffee in the history of everything ever. But no pressure."

"I have an espresso machine back at my place that will blow your mind."

Hour Twenty-Three

The early-dawn air feels brisk, biting, almost confrontational as we leave the warmth of the dojo and step onto the sidewalk. We walk at double-speed. The light is silvery-peach. A few buses rumble down the street, scantily filled with drowsy passengers, ears plugged with headphones. The city is flexing and yawning and stretching. Dawn is coming.

Within minutes, I'm seated in the exact same spot I found myself just a few hours earlier—reclining on Ren's couch, a discarded copy of *Wired* magazine by my side. He's busying himself in the kitchen. The oily resonance of freshly ground coffee fills the air. He turns to glance at me over his shoulder and smiles. I smile back.

The sweet, unhurried domesticity of this moment is so sweet, I almost cry. So normal. So perfectly couple-ish. I rise from the couch and float around the room without much direction, studying his possessions, idly stroking the top the couch, browsing through books and DVDs. Taking in the pieces of his world.

I notice a small vintage-looking radio resting on his desk. I flip it on, turning the dial from station to station, hunting for the perfect soundtrack for this moment.

A Christian rocker earnestly sings about sins being washed clean. Next. A rapper boasts about how many fine-ass booties be up in dis club. Next.

A trio of aggressively chipper morning talk show hosts deliver the salacious celebrity gossip of the day. Nope.

There's a chasm of static, and then I arrive on a familiar spot on the dial.

"It's 6 a.m., and you're listening to . . ."

It's one of my favorite public radio hosts. Her measured, dulcet voice evokes a thousand memories of a thousand mornings—listening to her report on the news of the hour while brushing my teeth, zipping my coat, readying myself for the day ahead. I'm lulled by the familiar intonation of her voice, and I pause, my hand resting on the desk as she continues with the morning news.

There's been another bombing in another country that, shamefully, I don't think I could spell correctly or locate on a world map. Civilians have been injured. The final death toll has not yet been tabulated. On a happier note: the Pope is visiting Japan and thoroughly enjoyed his visit to the Meiji Shrine in Tokyo. In other news: the offspring of the world's first cloned dolphin have all died for reasons unknown. But the whales are all doing well.

It's the usual blend of unthinkable violence, hesitant optimism, and glimmers of hope, delivered in a rapid succession of audio sound bites. After the fifth or sixth news update, I'm feeling saturated with information, and I'm just about to turn the dial, when . . .

"A new study from Cambridge University reveals exciting information about the procedure known as TCR, or Temporary Cellular Resuscitation."

Across the room, with a milk-frothing device in one hand, Ren turns swiftly to face me. Without saying a word, his message emanates clearly through every cell of his body:

"Don't turn it off." Immobilized, facing one another with approximately seventeen feet of empty space between us, we listen to the broadcast with rapt attention. The host continues her preamble.

"Commonly known as the 'bonus round,' TCR has been gaining popularity in recent years—with over 1.8 million customers in the past fiscal quarter alone. As most listeners may already know, the life-extending effects of TCR typically last for twenty-four hours. Sometimes slightly less, sometimes slightly more. But one research team may have discovered a surprising loophole. We turn, now, to Dr. Gerard Livingston for an update on the project. Dr. Livingston, thank you for joining us here today."

The host and research doctor exchange the usual pleasantries. *Thank you, the honor is all mine,* etcetera, and so forth. Ren and I wait with stiffened breath, willing them to cut to the chase.

"Dr. Livingston, you're the lead author of a new research paper that was published in the latest issue of the *British Medical Journal,* which was released just a few hours ago," the host continues. "Can you summarize your findings for our listeners?"

"Of course," the doctor responds, with that clipped British accent that every American immediately associates with "trustworthy professionalism and authority."

"My team at Cambridge has been studying the possibility of ECR, or Extended Cellular Resuscitation."

"Like an extended version of TCR?"

"That's right. Whereas the life-extending effects of TCR typically last for one day, my team is pursuing the possibility of extending that experience for two days, three, four, perhaps more."

"The goal being, to give people who have been temporarily resuscitated from death a little extra time," the host clarifies.

"That's right. A bit more time. When you're in that, ah, em, condition, two or three extra days can be a priceless gift."

I glance at Ren. His gaze is rooted to the floor, as if making eye contact with me would undo his carefully

sealed composure, shattering him into pieces. My
stomach is lurching, gyrating, as the broadcast continues.

"So what have you discovered? Is it possible to
extend life past the usual timeframe of twenty-four
hours?" the radio host asks. Her voice—usually so
controlled and purged of any discernible opinion—
betrays the subtlest hint of emotion. I wonder,
momentarily, if this radio host has purchased TCR for
herself—or for someone she loves. Because she wants to
know the answer. Badly. And so do I.

"The answer to that question is ... yes."

Ren's face glows like the sun. He lifts his gaze to
meet mine. But neither one of us smiles. We're both
waiting for the inevitable "But . . ." to drop like a
hammer. And it does.

"But . . ." the doctor continues. "Our research is
extremely preliminary, and to date, we have been unable
to replicate the occurrence."

"Can you describe the 'occurrence' that you
mentioned in your research paper?" The host presses.

Silently, Ren moves to my side and takes my hand
in his own. We stand, imprisoned in a cage of sound,
listening to two disembodied strangers discussing details
that may or may not directly impact my life. It's like I'm
an inmate on death row waiting to discover if I've been
pardoned. I'm tingling, uneasy, and desperately trying

to stamp out the soft scuffling of hope inside my heart
because hope feels much too dangerous.

The doctor quickly details his project.

One thousand mice. Fifty percent died of natural
causes. Fifty percent were killed by the researchers (he
said, "death was induced" but come on, we all know
what that means). TCR was administered to all of the
mice—*zing! they're back!*—and then the resuscitated mice
were divided into a variety of groups. Each group of
mice got pricked, prodded, infused, defibrillated, and
toyed with in a unique way—dozens of different ways
to possibly, maybe, theoretically extend life a few more
precious hours.

One group of mice received no additional treatment.

"That was, of course, the control group," Dr.
Livingston explains patronizingly.

"And within the control group," the host intervenes,
trying to move the story along.

"There was one mouse who exhibited, as you put it,
an 'atypical response.' "

"Correct. One mouse responded atypically to the
TCR procedure. We nicknamed this mouse Lazarus," the
doctor adds, chuckling at his own uncontainable wit and
brilliance. My temper is shortening. *Get to the point, doc.*
The host seems to share my impatience.

"Doctor, how long do mice typically remain alive
after TCR has been administered?"

"Typically a few minutes, at most."

"And this one mouse? The one you named Lazarus?"

There's a slow intake of breath, and a significant pause, as if the doctor can't believe what he's about to say:

"Eleven months."

There's another prolonged pause. Probably just a few seconds, but in radio-time, the vacancy feels like an eternity. Dr. Livingston's voice cuts the silence.

"To put that in perspective, if Lazarus were a human being rather than a mouse, that would equate to nearly fifty-six years."

"Fifty-six years of additional life?" The host exclaims. "But how?"

"Well," the doctor chirps brightly. "That is the big question, now, isn't it? As I mentioned earlier, our research is extremely preliminary. We cannot point to any particular reason why this mouse—this one mouse—continued to live, and live, and live, while the other test subjects did not. We are investigating numerous possibilities. For example, this atypical response could be due to a genetic abnormality. But there are dozens of other physiological factors that may or may not have played a role in this miracle occurrence. We simply don't have clear answers. Not yet."

"You're calling this a 'miracle?' " the host asks incredulously.

"A miracle is defined as an event that is not explicable by scientific laws," the doctor replies. "So yes, I would categorize this occurrence as a miracle."

Ren gives me a look filled with unbearable hope.

"Doctor, we have to wrap up this story shortly, but there's one other aspect of your research paper that I think our listeners will find very fascinating . . ."

And just like that, I can't stand hearing another word. I yank the radio out of the wall socket. The doctor's brisk, unctuous tone snips into nothingness.

Ren roars furiously.

"No! What? He was about to ... Why did you . . ."

He scrambles to plug the radio back into the wall, hands trembling and fumbling with the cord as he crouches near the floor. His eyes are inflamed, blazing gold.

"Why did you turn if off?" he asks, his voice steely and spine-chilling. "Don't you want to hear the rest? Don't you want to know?"

In this moment, the beautiful man that I love is hunched by the floor, still fumbling with the socket, overwrought with emotion. It's the first time I've seen him look ... ungraceful. I feel sickened, knowing that I did this to him, that I brought this nightmare into his life.

But I can't. I just can't.

"I don't want to hear anymore," I respond. "I don't want to know."

Daggers of dismay and pained confusion shoot from his eyes, piercing my heart.

"But why not?"

Nausea builds in my gut. Instead of vomiting bile, I vomit words.

"Because I don't want to get my hopes up!" I bark at him, not quite screaming but nearly. "Because I don't want to listen to some radio doctor talk about 'atypical responses' and 'preliminary findings' and 'miracles' like somehow it applies to me. Because it doesn't!"

My knees buckle, and I'm sinking down, sobbing and mucus-logged, down onto the ground with Ren, who's still clutching the plastic radio in his hands like somehow it can save us. It won't. I curl towards Ren, and he flinches at my touch. That one flinch—so subtle, almost imperceptible, just a ghost of rejection—is the most painful thing I've ever seen or felt. Worse than death.

I turn to him, pleading with every fiber of my being, trying to make him understand.

"I am not the freak mouse who miraculously lives," I choke-sob, crumpled on his lap. "I don't want to get all hopeful and gooey-eyed and pretend like that. It's delusional, OK? Don't you get it? It hurts too much."

He sets the radio onto the ground and kicks it away with a free leg, pulling me into his arms. I grip his arms, so relieved to be welcomed back home into his embrace. It's like air after being held underwater. It's like sunlight after losing yourself in a cavernous underground tunnel. It's like life.

"I get it," he says. "I respect your choice. I really do." The beastly fury has melted out of his voice. "Thank you for agreeing with me."

"I didn't say that I agreed with you," he counters. "I don't agree. If it were up to me, I'd be listening to the rest of that radio broadcast, then Googling to find the research paper they mentioned, and then buying a plane ticket to England to meet that doctor in person, with a list of about a hundred questions that I want to ask him. Because if there were any chance—even if it's the smallest chance—that you could somehow stay alive for another fifty-six years, or even another fifty-six hours, I would pursue that chance until the edges of the world. I would want to know. I would NEED to know."

It's the most romantic thing I've ever heard. I can just picture it—Ren, boarding a flight to London, racing to catch the train to Cambridge, marching into that doctor's research facility, demanding answers to unanswerable questions. It's romantic. Romantic and stupid. Because the answers don't exist. The doctor said it himself—the mouse survived and nobody knows

why. An unexplainable miracle. An atypical response.
No answers.

Besides, I'll be gone before Ren even boards the
plane. There's absolutely no time. Whatever miracle
struck that research facility in Cambridge is not going to
strike this one-bedroom apartment in Minneapolis.

Romantic, stupid, and heartbreakingly sweet.

"I am not the freak mouse . . ." I repeat again softly, as
much to myself as to him.

He holds me and says nothing more. He doesn't
have to. As his breathing synchronizes with mine,
as the powdery-pink light of the rising sun fills the
room, I know exactly what he's wondering. What
he's allowing himself to hope for, even though it's
ridiculous, even though it's only setting him up for
inevitable disappointment.

But what if you could be ... ?

Hour Twenty-Four

"How about that cup of coffee?" I ask, offering a weak smile. "I was promised 'mind-blowing espresso,' if I recall correctly."

Ren hops dutifully to his feet, heading back over to the machine he abandoned during the news broadcast. Within moments, I am presented with a perfectly frothed latte in a sky blue cup. He has designed a swirling pattern in the foam, something like a cross between a heart and a maple leaf. It's impressive.

"You've got skills . . ." I say, and the compliment makes him glow with pride. In this moment, he reminds me of a lion cub—proud and strong but also yearning for my undivided attention and praise. It's a cute combination.

"I may have watched a few YouTube tutorials," he says, by way of explanation.

"Awww. You really need to get a life."

He laughs and nods. "You're probably right about that. After teaching six or seven classes at the dojo, and then doing my own workout for the day, I'm usually totally exhausted. I tend to grab something for dinner on my way home, and then I just read in bed or watch YouTube clips or Netflix the rest of the night. I'm usually asleep by 9:30 p.m.," he grimaces, as if this information is flat-out embarrassing. "I'm basically a senior citizen."

I can picture Ren tucked in bed, hair loose and freshly showered, gray and white sheets tousled all around, watching a show on his laptop. Maybe some type of show that guys love—something with car chases or drug lords or dragons. Maybe all of the above. Maybe he finishes off his night by masturbating—reaching into his bedside drawer to retrieve the bottle of lube that I suspect is hidden there, working himself into a frenzy, then sinking luxuriously into sleep.

So normal. So ordinary. So boring—but in a completely beautiful way.

I imagine a different variation of that same night—both of us showering together, crawling into bed, play-fighting over which show to watch, perching my laptop on a pillow at just the right angle. I curl into the safety of his body, resting my head on his chest, and he absentmindedly twirls a lock of my damp hair with his fingers, using his free hand to hit: *Play.* The silvery-blue glow of the screen illuminates our faces. Dragons roar, swords clash, and kings rage onto the battlefield, fighting for their family's name, land, and honor ... And later there's kissing. And maybe popcorn. We descend into sleep with our arms interlocked, legs tangled, and when I wake up he's the first thing I see ...

I close my eyes and allow myself to revel in this fantasy. Somehow, it feels sexier than almost anything I can imagine. Deliciously ordinary. TV and touching and clean sheets and sleep. The type of moment that most happy couples take entirely for granted.

"Another one?" Ren asks, noticing my empty coffee mug. I shake my head.

"I'm good."

"Want to see something cool?"

He's beaming like a kid who just discovered how to mix baking soda and vinegar to create a volcano in the sink.

"Totally."

He springs up from the couch and paces briskly towards the door.

"Come on."

We move down the hallway towards the eastern side of the building. Dawn is in full bloom. Golden light pours through the small window at the end of the hall. The sky is turning from rose to blue, streaked with transparent clouds that trail off like comets.

After a few paces, he stops and gestures towards the wall. There's a ladder. Old and partially rusted, but sturdy enough.

"It goes up to the roof," he explains, already climbing upwards. I follow. At the top, there's a door that swings upward. It's unlocked and swings open easily like the cover of a book. A cool early-morning breeze greets us as we climb through the opening.

It's clear that he's been here before. There's a yoga mat unfurled on the roof. Next to that, a metal chest. He pops it open to reveal another mat, a blanket, and several pillows. Working quickly, he arranges everything beautifully to create—for the second time today, or possibly the third—a pillow-nest. A soft place for us to land.

The roof has a subtle tilt to allow rainwater to drain off the edge, but it's mostly flat. We recline on our backs, side by side, and we're in our own kingdom of light and clouds, invisible to the rest of the world.

"There was a time in my life when I wanted to die."

Ren's voice cuts through the idyllic, dreamlike quality of this moment. I curl my fingers through his, unsure if—or how—I should respond to this abrupt and strange statement. Gray pigeons circle overhead and somewhere, several stories below, a bicycle bell chimes. In the end, I don't have to say anything, because he continues to speak.

"I was nineteen. Everything in my life felt so sharp and ugly. My girlfriend had dumped me—cheated on me with my best friend, actually, and then lied to me about it. It felt like the worst kind of betrayal. Then right after that, I performed terribly at a national karate tournament and it was humiliating. Instead of feeling

motivated to train harder, I just blamed everyone else—
my sensei, the panel of judges, my opponent."

I listen silently, wishing I could time-travel back to
that tournament to comfort him, even though there's
probably nothing I could have done or said to alleviate
his pain: the unique pain of tasting defeat—crushing,
public, ego-shattering defeat—for the very first time.
Older, wiser adults can offer you all types of inspiring
pep talks and motivational slogans but at nineteen?
You're deaf to it all. You don't believe a word of it.
Grown-ups are blathering idiots, and the only thing that
feels real is your pain. I remember.

"But that was really just the surface stuff. The truth
is that I didn't think my life was worth anything. I wasn't
that good at school, just average. I wasn't that good at
martial arts, just average. Maybe slightly above average
but not good enough to win a national title. I wasn't
'excellent' at anything. Oh, and I had really bad acne back
then. Like really, really bad. I know it's vain and stupid,
but every time I looked in the mirror, I hated what I saw.
It really wrecked me."

It's hard for me to imagine Ren as an awkward,
late-adolescent, not-quite-adult man with pustules
covering his skin, filled with anger and acidic blame,
roiling with unmanaged testosterone. Compared with
the calm, beautiful man resting beside me, it feels like

he's describing a completely different person. Not just
another person—another species.

"One night after sparring practice at the dojo—
which went terribly—I was walking home, crossing
the Stone Arch Bridge. Just thinking about how much
I hated my skin, hated my ex, hated my life. Thinking
about how it felt like there was nothing to look forward
to, nothing on the horizon … I reached the center of
the bridge and I stopped. I stared into the water down
below. It was white and frothy, almost like rapids, and
I imagined myself disappearing beneath the surface.
Just falling, sinking, forever. It wasn't that I wanted to
die, exactly … it was more like, I didn't want to feel so
disgusted with myself anymore. I didn't want to feel
anything at all. I just wanted to feel … nothing."

"Then what happened?" I can't stop myself
from interjecting.

The sun is growing warmer, and I kick off the
blanket. His eyes are closed. I stroke his forearm gently,
and a smile spreads across his face.

"What happened is that … I stared at the water
for a while. I thought about jumping. I mean, I really,
seriously, considered it. What would it feel like? Would
it hurt? Would my legs snap? Or my neck? Would I feel
regret as I'm falling—or just relief? If my bones break,
would I bleed from the inside? Or would I be knocked

unconscious instantly, asleep and unfeeling as I sink into the water . . ."

I shiver in spite of the sunlight. Gruesome images ricochet through my mind. I've never been on the brink of suicide, not even close, and it's hard to wrap my head around what that must be like. What it's like to feel that level of hopelessness and pain.

"And then," he continues. "I notice two people walking beneath the bridge. A man and a woman. They were on that little island-like area by the reservoir. I could see them walking together, linking arms. I couldn't hear them because of the sound of the water, but I could tell they were smiling, laughing. She tilted her head back to the sky, like he'd said something so funny she couldn't stand it. They sort of skip-walked over to this area where, I guess, they thought nobody could see them. It was almost nighttime. And then she looks over her shoulder. And then she sinks down to her knees. And then—now, OK, bear in mind they're pretty far away from me, and it's getting dark—but I am pretty damn sure she's giving him a blowjob. Like a fast, secret, naughty sort of public blowjob. I mean, what else could it be? And he leans against the barricade, and his hands are all lost in her hair and he's smiling. Like, smiling so big, I can see it from the top of the bridge. Like this is the best moment of his life, and he literally can't believe how lucky he is."

"Oh my god … wait, what?" I exclaim. This is not where I thought this story was going. I'm bubbling over with about a million questions, but I stifle myself, allowing him to finish.

"And I see this guy's face, and I think to myself, *OK, maybe my life isn't always going to suck. Maybe one day, I can get a blowjob underneath a bridge from a beautiful woman on a nice summer night. Because that would be awesome.*"

There's a pause. I'm waiting for him to add something more to the story. Some deep spiritual revelation. Some profound personal epiphany. Some pivotal realization that changed everything and careened his life in a new direction. But there's nothing more. That's the story. *"Because that would be awesome."* The end.

I know it's inappropriate. I kind of hate myself for doing it. But I can't help it—I start laughing. Just a few nervous giggles at first. And then—to my great relief— he joins me.

"So let me get this straight," I recap. "You're nineteen years old, you're suicidal, you're standing on top of the bridge ready to jump, but then you see some dude getting an awesome blowjob, and you're like, *'That looks nice. Maybe I should give this 'life' thing another shot'? That's* what happened? Just like that?"

"Pretty much," he replies.

"That is so … so … weird and sad and amazing."

"We should start an indie band together and write a #1 hit song called 'Weird and Sad and Amazing,'" he tells me, smiling in that way that you smile when you're suppressing a laugh, but then you can't stifle yourself any longer and ... out it comes.

"Duh, absolutely."

Our banter melts into giggles, giggles taper off into sighs, and then silence. I roll over onto my stomach, pressing myself closer to Ren so that every possible square inch of my body is connected with his.

"Why did you tell me that weird, sad, and amazing story?" I ask. "If it's because you're hinting that you want a blowjob right now, um . . ."

"Is that an offer?" he interjects, with complete seriousness. His face is serene, but his eyes glint with mischief, and I know he's just teasing me. At least, mostly. Like seventy percent teasing, thirty percent totally down for it. He looks so regal and inviting right now, outstretched in the sunlight—honestly, he wouldn't have to ask twice.

He props himself up on his elbows, and the mischief melts out of his eyes.

"I told you that weird, sad, and amazing story because I want you to know that I'm so glad I didn't jump off that bridge. I'm glad I changed my mind. And after that day, I'm glad I got therapy. I'm glad I learned how to take better care of my brain. I'm glad I decided to stay on the planet. I'm glad for about a million different reasons—and one of those reasons is because I got the chance to meet you."

I climb on top of him, straddling him with my back to the sunlight, because after a declaration like that, how could I not?

"I'm glad you decided to stay on the planet, too," I reply, covering his neck with a trail of kisses.

I feel a thrilling, stiff pressure at the place where our bodies connect. And then—because we're in love, because I'm about to die, because we're currently alive, because it's fun, because it's sacred, because everything is ending, because it's all a big disaster, because this is probably the last chance ever, I peel down the top of his pants, cover his mouth with mine, and pull him inside. I move slowly. He pulls my hips down further, deeper, and I'm crying, and he's crying too, and it's all just a beautiful mess. Weird, sad, and amazing.

I wring everything out of my body until I'm empty, so empty, emptier than I've ever been. My cheek hits his chest, and it's the most perfect resting place, blissful and silky soft, like resting on a beach that has been warmed by the sun. His heartbeat is the tide, lapping in, lapping out. He's touching my hair, telling me *I love you, I love you, I love you,* over and over, hypnotically serenading me, pulling me under.

I roll onto my back and he's above me, covering me with more kisses. The last thing I see are his eyes, deep brown, molten hazel-honey, framed by dark lashes, framed by his skin, framed by the sky. Sky to eyes, it's a bullseye of powder blue fading inward to the deepest brown and green—green like the trees by the falls where we swam that first time. He smiles and says *I love you* once again. He says it with his lips, and then he says it with his entire body as he pulls me close, so close that I'm fading into him. Fading in and out and in.

I want to stay here but I am so tired. Ten miles beyond tired, fighting for consciousness but losing the battle. My thoughts dissolve into particles of nothingness, and then there are no more words at all. My eyelids are heavy, dropping down, closing like curtains. Falling, closing, and then the world is just a slice of light.

The last thing I feel is his arm slipping under my neck, cradling my head.

So this is the end.

Epilogue

— *Ren* —

I held her and she was there.

I held her and she wasn't there.

I don't know how else to describe it.

Nora's eyes closed slowly, almost in slow motion, like she was drinking in every last sliver of light and savoring each ray. So slowly, narrowing and narrowing, and then ... nothing.

I watched her ribcage rise and fall a few more times, and I whispered my love for her with every inhalation, as if my words could fill her lungs. Then her breathing became so faint that I couldn't tell if she was alive or dead. And then she was gone. Just like that.

It was a soft and peaceful exit from this world, as gentle as anyone could wish for. But I didn't wish for this.

In books, movies and snatches of conversations, I've overheard people say things like, "When such-and-such happened, a part of me died."

It's a flippant turn of phrase. The person speaking usually doesn't mean it. Not really. It's just a commonly used exaggeration.

This is no exaggeration for me.

Watching her fade away, a part of me died. I mean *really* died.

That feeling you get when you're running too fast down a flight of stairs and you miss a step and begin to fall—that split second of gut-flipping panic and disorientation when you're hovering in mid-air between two steps with no footing—imagine that sensation crashing through your body, over and over and over, with no reprieve. Hollowness. Anguish. Animalistic terror. Screaming with no sound, like in a terrible dream.

I wanted to fling myself into whatever tunnel she was walking through.

I wanted to follow her into the light, into the cosmos, wherever she was going.

This was my first confrontation with death—with someone I actually care about—and I've discovered, to my shame, that I am completely unprepared. Like a child wandering through a carnival that is too loud and too bright, unattended and afraid. Like a wanderer with a broken compass, I am lost. I don't know what to do with any of this.

I don't even know what to do with her body.

Partly because the sun is growing uncomfortably warm, and partly because I don't know what else to do next, I fold Nora over my shoulders and carry her from the rooftop back down to my apartment, silently praying that nobody sees us. Because I don't really know how I'd explain any of this to my neighbors. *"It's cool, guys. It's not what it looks like."* I can only imagine their horrified, stunned expressions. Followed by an immediate 911 call that would probably end with me in handcuffs.

Back in the apartment, I arrange her on my bed. My heart is pounding with exertion—carrying a woman down multiple flights of stairs is no easy task, regardless of how fit you are—and I pace back and forth across my bedroom, catching my breath and running through my options.

Am I supposed to call the hospital? Call the morgue? She gave me a handful of letters.

Am I supposed to read them? Did she leave instructions inside?

I reach into my pocket and withdraw one, two, three folded pieces of paper. One for her mother. One for that woman she told me about, Tasha. One for me.

For me.

I didn't realize she wrote a letter for me.

I tear it open hungrily, willing myself to read it slowly, to draw it out, and make it last. But of course I don't have that kind of self-control, not right now, and I devour it greedily.

Ren,

Call Abbott Central Hospital. Give them your address. They'll come to collect me.

Please donate everything in my apartment to charity. Or Craigslist or whatever. Or keep some stuff if you want. There's really not much in there. (I wrote my address on the back of this letter, FYI.)

I don't have that much money in my bank account, but whatever's in there, it should go to my mom for her nursing care. I already filled out the form at my bank—a couple years ago—to make her my "payable-on-death" beneficiary, so there shouldn't be any trouble with the transfer. But maybe call the nursing home, and let them know what's up. Thanks. Also, please tell my mom that I love her.

OK. That's all the logistical stuff, I think. Obviously I should have written an official last will and testament— notarized and everything—but it's one of those things that I always postponed until "someday later," like most people do. So, I'm sorry to burden you with all those errands. I hope it's not too much to deal with.

The real point of this letter is to tell you that I have fallen in love with you. You own my heart. I know I already told you, but now you have physical proof, ink and paper:

I love you.

Thank for you reminding me—showing me—what it feels like to be alive.

A part of me hopes you will remember the time that we shared forever, that you'll fondly remember me on your deathbed many, many years from now. That you'll never get over me. Not ever.

But another part of me (the less selfish part) hopes that you'll move on with your life very quickly—meet a beautiful woman, maybe at Voltage Coffee, or maybe she'll wander into the dojo one afternoon and sign up for a beginner level Aikido class. You'll feel that incredible spark. You'll ask her out on a date. You'll kiss her. She'll kiss you back. You'll take a sunset stroll, arm in arm, looping around Lake Calhoun, and everything will feel so simple and true. You'll get married and have a zillion babies (or not, if you don't want to) and live the fullest, richest life imaginable. That's what I really hope for you. Because that's the life you deserve.

I love you, Ren.

I love you, but I'm not saying goodbye.

You told me that you believe in reincarnation—some variety of it, anyway—so wherever I am going, I will meet you there.

Nora

I read it over and over and over and over and over and then … one more time.

I know it's wrong. It's seriously creepy, actually. But I'm so in love with this woman that I need to feel her lips on mine. Just one more time.

My nose grazes her cheek, my lips claim her mouth, because even now, even like this, she's still mine.

Please don't judge me for this, for what I'm about to say next. Unless you've lost someone you love, then you don't understand the illogical, hysterical grief that overtakes you. The senseless behavior that follows. Because next, what I do is … I talk to her. All day long. I talk to her, and I stroke her hair, and I refill my glass of water, and I encircle us with blankets, like we're savoring a lazy weekend together and everything is perfectly normal.

I talk to her and I imagine her reactions, even though she's motionless and cold. Even though I know she can't hear me. Even though I know she's gone.

I tell her about my dreams for the dojo, how I'd love to expand the business, what I envision myself doing in five or ten years. I tell her about my dream of becoming a father, and how finally I'm at a point in my life where that feels like a responsible, viable possibility. I tell her about my favorite action movies, and my most secret of all secret guilty pleasures, which is that I really love watching home renovation TV shows where they take a fixer-upper and turn it into something absolutely stunning. Sometimes I'll watch three or four episodes in a row, fantasizing about my future home . . .

I talk and I talk. My stomach rumbles but I don't eat. The sky outside darkens but I don't care. I talk and I cry and I talk more, filling hours with my stories and recollections.

I'm just not ready to say goodbye. Not ready to watch strangers carry her out of my home, out of my sight, never to return. I don't think I'll ever be ready for that, and I want to postpone the agony of that moment until . . . well, basically until forever.

I curl up close to her body, facing her with our knees touching. Then I shift up just a few inches so that her cheek rests on my chest. Something leaves my body, something silent and convulsive, halfway between a sob and a sigh. Eventually I'll call the hospital.

Eventually. But not yet. Hollow and stricken, I close my eyes.

There's a flutter.

So faint, I almost miss it.

Eyelashes on my collarbone.

My eyes snap open in shock. For a moment, I'm convinced I'm hallucinating.

"Am I still here?" Nora asks hoarsely. Her eyes flicker open, puzzled and searching. "Is this . . . how long . . . I don't . . ."

Before I can say anything, I need to kiss her again. I need to. I can't not. Her legs clasp behind me and she wriggles into me, feeling warm, humanly warm, soft and yielding.

"Ren, what happened? How long was I … ?" she asks softly, drifting into bewildered silence.

"Nora, it's been nine hours. Nine hours, Nora. Nine. Nine. Nine." I am repeating myself, fully aware that I sound psychotic. But I can't suppress my shock and elation.

Nine hours have passed since the twenty-four-hour mark when she was supposed to die, permanently. And yet somehow she's here. She's back. She was cold. Now she's warm. She was gone. Now there's hope. Like the comatose man who regained the ability to speak after twenty years of complete paralysis. Like the boy submerged in freezing water for forty-three minutes who didn't die. Like the magician who buried himself alive and escaped. Like the creation of the universe. Like Lazarus rising from the grave. Like every miracle, like every great mystery, there is no way of knowing exactly, "How?" There is no neat and tidy explanation. Only wonder. And gratitude. Unending gratitude.

Everything seems impossible until it happens for the first time.

Twenty-four plus nine equals thirty-three hours in total. That's more, way more, than any TCR has ever lasted before. I'm pretty certain that's a world record.

"Am I the lucky freak mouse?" she asks me, so softly and roughly, barely more than a whisper.

"I think, possibly, you might be. How do you feel?"

I help her into a sitting position. She stares outward, facing my bedroom window, considering the darkening late afternoon sky with curiosity, as if she's not quite convinced that any of this is real.

Gently brushing my hands aside, she lifts herself onto her feet. She walks towards the edge of the rooftop. She looks up. She seems to be staring into nothing and into everything. I look up, too, taking in the outline of a faint, marbled moon. The spaces in between the branches of the trees where the light peeks through. The rippling of the breeze, that silky motion of leaves shifting left, shifting right.

I want to explode with questions. But I say nothing, letting this moment be quiet and still.

She takes a few steps to the right. I spring immediately to her side, arms outstretched protectively, just in case she falters or wobbles.

She doesn't.

"Ren … it's OK. I feel fine. Like, completely fine. Really thirsty, but otherwise, fine."

She turns to face me, her eyes wide and wondering, pupils dilated, two inky gemstones. I can read the unspoken questions in every curve and line of her face.

How did this happen? What does this mean?

And then, there's that other unspoken question— the one that has haunted us practically since the moment we met.

And how much time is left?

I don't know. She doesn't know. Dr. Livingston at the Cambridge Medical Research Facility in England doesn't know. Nobody knows. Human beings, with our procedures, tabulations, predictions, and our wild, egotistical assurance. We always think we know. And sometimes we do. But then sometimes we don't.

I move to her side, burying my face in her dark, silky hair. It smells like blueberries and waterfalls and coffee and the pillows on my bed. Like the city suspended around us.

And like home.

"Now what?" I ask, because I genuinely don't know. "What do we do now?"

She takes my hand in hers. She's already moving down the ladder, down into my building, down towards the hallway that leads out into the rest of the world. She laces her fingers with mine and she tells me:

"We go live."

A Note from the Author

I have a friend who remembers all of her dreams. She wakes up at four or five in the morning, most days, and she records her dreams in a journal. She has collected over 80,000 words so far. Some people have that ability, you know? The ability to bolt awake in bed and remember everything that just happened.

I am not one of those people.

I almost never remember my dreams, and when I do, it's usually an unbelievably boring situation. Like, a dream where I'm reviewing an Excel spreadsheet, or a dream where I'm answering an email and then (gasp, oh the horror!) I notice a typo. That sort of thing.

But one night, something happened that I'd never experienced before.

I woke up in the middle of the night, abruptly, like I'd been ripped into consciousness. I felt feverish and disoriented. My heart was pounding as if I'd been sprinting uphill and I was crying, but I didn't know why.

I felt Brandon's presence behind me, warm and solid, and that comforted me. My heart rate began to slow down. I exhaled. And then, suddenly, I remembered everything.

I remembered the entire dream I'd just had while I was sleeping. I could see every single detail, like it was a movie replaying in my head.

In the dream, I had died. And somehow, doctors brought me back to life. A second chance. But they warned me, "This will only last for one day. Twenty-four hours."

Throughout the dream, I navigated my final day. I remember feeling a powerful, almost unbearable sense of urgency. It was like a pressure on my chest, a feeling of anxiety coupled with a desire to make every moment count. Time was passing too quickly. Everything was sharp, intense, and bittersweet. I hugged my parents and didn't want to let go. I laid down on the grass with Brandon, pressed my skin close to his, and desperately wished we could have just a little bit longer, just a few more moments.

Inside the dream, I remember feeling so grateful for this second chance. Grateful, but, at the same time, frightened and heartbroken. Because I knew, "This is the end." There was nothing I could do to hold back time, to stop the inevitable ending from coming. And I wasn't ready to say goodbye.

I still cry when I think about that dream. I cry every time. I wish I were a more talented writer so that I could convey, fully, how much it impacted me.

For me, this dream was a wake-up call. It felt like God, Spirit, the Universe, whatever term you prefer, was shaking me awake and saying:

"This is your one and only life. *This is it.* And I hate to break it to you, but this ride could end at any moment. So, go live. Really live. Appreciate each day. Savor every moment. Don't waste time. Don't sleepwalk, text, email, and tweet your way through your life. Don't just stare at a digital screen for twelve hours a day. Don't just exist. *Be alive.*"

That dream was the inspiration behind the book. I hope you enjoyed Nora and Ren's love story. I hope it inspires you to make a special meal for your sweetheart tonight, and say "I love you" and really mean it, and hold your kids close, and take a spontaneous trip with a friend instead of postponing it until next year, and turn off your phone and look up into the night sky, and really *feel* your life.

If you had exactly twenty-four hours remaining in the story of your life, what would you do?

What would matter? What wouldn't matter at all? What would you miss the most about this world? Would it be the smell of pancakes on Sunday morning? The feeling of freshly laundered sheets on your bed? The quiet satisfaction that comes from finishing a tough, sweaty workout? Beach days, camping trips, friends and cold beers around the fire pit, or the pulse of your favorite music? Curling your fingers through your partner's hand as you meander through the aisles of the grocery store? What are the moments you love most?

Let's try, as best we can, to fill our lives with those kinds of moments and appreciate them fully. Today is here. Tomorrow is never guaranteed. The end is always coming. There's no time to waste.

Book Club
Discussion Questions

1. At the beginning of the story, Nora wakes up in a hospital bed. She has received Temporary Cellular Resuscitation (TCR), which has temporarily revived her body, giving her an extra twenty-four hours of life—like re-charging a battery. If a procedure like TCR existed in real life, would you want to do it? Why or why not?

2. If you were creating a list called *"Things to Do During My Final Twenty-Four Hours of Life,"* what would be on that list? What would definitely *not* be on that list?

3. After waking up in the hospital, Nora reaches for her phone to announce her death on Facebook. If you were in her position, would you do the same thing? Why or why not? What's your feeling on social media? Do you think it plays too big of a role in our lives?

4. Nora's story takes an exciting turn after she meets Tasha, the woman who pushes her to create an online dating profile and go on a first date. Do you have a "Tasha" in your own life—someone who pushes you out of your comfort zone, who nudges

you to take risks that you wouldn't normally take? Who is that person for you?

5. Nora and Ren both feel an immediate connection and fall in love very quickly. Do you think it's possible to really be "in love" with someone after just a few hours? Have you ever experienced that? Or do you think it's unrealistic?

6. The ending of the story is somewhat ambiguous. Nora appears to be alive once again, but for how long? Minutes? Hours? Years? What do you think the ending means? What do you think happens next for Nora and Ren?

7. Did this story inspire you to call your parents, hug your kids, kiss your partner, or approach your life differently in some way? What's your takeaway or *"aha"* moment from this story?

Thank You

Brandon. I hope we get reincarnated together a million times.

Mom and Dad. Thanks for having sex in Mexico so that I could be born! Good job!

Ben and Olivia. How is it possible that I got the most amazing mom and dad … and *also* the best brother and sister? I love you guys so much.

Melissa and Nicole. Our email conversations make me cackle with laughter. You're both so inspiring to me, and I'm honored to be your friend.

Dyana. You always say to me, *"I'm glad you're on the planet."* I'm glad you're on the planet, too.

David Wagner. Your book, *Life As a Daymaker,* changed my life.

David Blaine. We've never met, but your magic makes me believe that anything is possible. You inspire me greatly.

RuPaul. We've never met, either, but you're one of the biggest influences in my life. From you, I learned that *"we're all born naked, and the rest is drag."* Life is a blank canvas. We can shape ourselves into anything we want.

Google. Thanks for all the info on cardiac arrest, Cambridge, Minneapolis street maps, and other stuff that I didn't know and/or forgot. You're seriously the smartest.

Spotify. I'd be lost without you! Thanks for the endless supply of music. (I made a playlist while writing this book and listened to it almost constantly. It's at http://bit.ly/so-this-is-the-end-playlist.)

My newsletter and blog readers. For almost a decade, I've shared personal stories (and sometimes, fictional stories) online. I'm blessed to have the most supportive, compassionate, and enthusiastic Internet family. Thanks for rolling with me.

You. Oh my gosh! You read my book? For real? That's surreal and amazing. Thank you. I hope you enjoyed it.

Alexandra Franzen

Alexandra Franzen is a writer based in Portland, Oregon, where she lives with her sweetheart Brandon and a dog named Dudley.

Her writing has been featured in places like *TIME*, *Forbes*, *Newsweek*, *The Huffington Post*, and *Lifehacker*. She's been mentioned in places like *The New York Times Small Business Blog*, *The Atlantic*, and *Inc*.

Alexandra writes a free weekly newsletter where she shares personal stories and thoughts on creativity, dealing with adversity, taking risks, building courage, designing a meaningful life, and how to create a positive ripple in the world. It's been praised as *"One of the 14 newsletters you need in your inbox"* by *Brit+Co*.

You'll find info about Alexandra's newsletter, books, and upcoming events at: AlexandraFranzen.com

"It is not death that a man should fear, but he should fear never beginning to live."

—Marcus Aurelius

Mango Publishing, established in 2014, publishes an eclectic list of books by diverse authors—both new and established voices—on topics ranging from business, personal growth, women's empowerment, LGBTQ studies, health, and spirituality to history, popular culture, time management, decluttering, lifestyle, mental wellness, aging, and sustainable living. We were recently named 2019 *and* 2020's #1 fastest-growing independent publisher by *Publishers Weekly.* Our success is driven by our main goal, which is to publish high-quality books that will entertain readers as well as make a positive difference in their lives.

Our readers are our most important resource; we value your input, suggestions, and ideas. We'd love to hear from you—after all, we are publishing books for you!

Please stay in touch with us and follow us at:
Facebook: Mango Publishing
Twitter: @MangoPublishing
Instagram: @MangoPublishing
LinkedIn: Mango Publishing
Pinterest: Mango Publishing
Newsletter: mangopublishinggroup.com/newsletter

Join us on Mango's journey to reinvent publishing, one book at a time.